I0452815

DAY OF THE GIANTS

DAY OF THE GIANTS

GIANTS

LESTER DEL REY

Includes the bonus story "The One-Eyed Man"

WILDSIDE PRESS

*Special thanks to Harv Millman and
Tom Horsley for proofing help.*

The Day of the Giants is copyright © 1959, 1987 by Lester del
Rey. (Copyright renewal #RE0000365076.) A shorter version
of this book was previously published as "When the World
Tottered" in *Fantastic Adventures*, December 1950.
"The One-Eyed Man" is copyright © 1945 by Street & Smith,
renewed 1973. Originally published in *Astounding Science
Fiction*, May 1945, under the pseudonym "Philip St. John."
All rights reserved.

CONTENTS

A NOTE FROM THE PUBLISHER

Wildside Press has been publishing great science fiction and fantasy since 1987. We have continued to grow and expand into many other genres, until today we are one of the largest "small presses" in the world.

Over the years, we have purchased the estates of a number of classic authors, including Lester del Rey, Mack Reynolds, Carl Jacobi, Reginald Bretnor, and others. We are working hard to digitize all their works and bring them out in new editions. (And sometimes we work with other publishers to bring these works out.)

If you enjoy the stories of Lester del Rey, watch for more new releases coming soon. Many additional titles are on the way.

—John Betancourt
Publisher, Wildside Press
wldsidepress.com | bcmystery.com

CHAPTER I

An Axe-age, a Sword-age, shields shall be cloven;
A Wind-age, a Wolf-age, ere the world totters.
                                                    —VÖLUSPA

Summer had ended before it began in June, and the first killing frost had come early in August. Now it was September, and winter was roaring across the fertile plains of the United States. Most of the crops had failed to ripen, and the only harvest on the farm lands was that of wood—there was a frantic race to cut wood for the stoves and furnaces that had to be kept full in the struggle against the cold.

Leif Svensen threw the last split log against the saw, feeding it automatically by the whine of the blade. He was a big, lean man, whose economy of motion made him seem slower than he was. The steel-blue eyes, blond hair and sharp-planed handsomeness must have come from some Viking ancestor, but there was none of the traditional sea rover's lust for living on his face. Only grim, dogged weariness showed now. He stacked the wood neatly and shut off the tractor motor, beating his hands together to warm them. Now he could hear the rising drone of the wind and the pinging of icy crystals on the metal roof above him. He scowled, not bothering to put on a smile as he turned toward the visitor who had been waiting for him to finish.

"Any recent news, Summers?" he asked, but there was no expectation in his voice. It had become a purely routine question.

"Radio says things are getting worse, that's all. There's a blizzard running from Dakota clear down to Kentucky. Guess we're just getting the edge of it now. Helluva year. Old man Erikson claims it's the end of the world." Summers gnawed at the corner of a plug of tobacco. There was a shadow of dull fear on his face, overlaying his habitual attempt at an ingratiating smile. He waited for encouragement, then sighed reluctantly. "Reason I come by, Leif, was about your dog. You changed your mind yet?"

"No," Leif answered flatly. "What I told the sheriff still goes. Rex has been chained up constantly for two weeks now, and I'm not letting anyone kill him for what some other animal does. Why should I?"

Summers cleared his throat awkwardly. "Now look, I ain't saying you should. I just figured I'd better warn you that the neighbors are holding an action meeting in the schoolhouse at five today. Al Storm says that two more of his pigs got killed last night by your dog or a wolf—and nobody's ever seen any wolves around here. He's mighty put out, Leif. Losing food like that ain't funny now. So I thought I'd best tell you about it. Might be better you should go to the meeting, talk to them before they decide on something foolish. They're pretty het up."

Leif's scowl deepened. Summers was right, of course. With the loss of fodder and crops over the whole world, there was a growing crisis in food; vigilantes were coming back into style in many places, and there had already been lynchings for less than the loss of a pig.

"Thanks," he said. "I'll try to get there. Know anything else?"

Summers' face brightened with sudden importance, but the fear was still there. "Seen an angel last night. On the level. Big blonde woman on a white horse, about a hundred feet up in the air, going hellbent east and singing loud enough to raise the dead. Just like the ones all the soldiers over there have been reporting. We were out hunting—four of us—long about sundown, if there'd been a sun, and we all seen her…Of course, there was supposed to be one over in Twin Forks last week, but…"

Leif let him ramble on, not surprised by it, but trying to pretend interest. Every period of war has its mass hallucinations, and the bitter stalemate that had begun in Europe was loaded with the hysteria of the weather and the fear of famine to come. Nobody had yet begun using atomic weapons, mercifully, but the tension of dread remained. It was small wonder that reports kept coming back of angels riding the sky on horseback over the battlefields—and lately, even here. The nonsense about flying saucers had just begun to quiet down after the first successful lunar probe revealed no aliens on the moon; now the crackpots were seeing angels instead. Summers' sighting had probably been only a trick cloud, catching a stray ray of sunshine, but there was no use in robbing the man of his importance by suggesting that.

Leif welcomed the sound of the phone from the house when his ears caught it during a lull in the wind. He started out at a run, throwing words over his shoulder to Summers. No knowing how long it had been ringing.

It was still ringing when he grabbed it up, though, and the voice of his win brother came from the receiver. "About time, Leif. How soon can you pick me up?"

"What happened to your motorcycle?"

"Skidded into the telephone pole at Five Corners. Not much left of the machine, but I jumped in time. Few scrapes and bruises, but it could be worse. A lot worse!" The phone carried the sound of a low chuckle as he muttered something away from the mouthpiece.

"I told you not to take that damned motorcycle out on these roads... Leif began, but Lee cut him off, still chuckling.

"So you did, son, so you did. Look, I'm at the Faulkner place, getting myself bandaged up. Know where it is? Good. Then come and collect your erring brother—but don't hurry too much. You should see what I've found for a nurse!"

The phone went dead, and Leif swore. Then he grinned wryly, with a mental picture of the bandaging that Lee would be enjoying. Lee was his twin's mental opposite. The crazy fool had managed to get into the Second World War at fifteen, had followed that with a trick in Korea, down into some South American fracas, and over half the known world. His letters had come back now and then, filled with exploits, women, casual citations and disgraces, more women, and sometimes money that Leif regarded with suspicion but had used to develop their farm.

Now Lee Svensen was back to recover from a chest wound he'd picked up two months before as a mercenary in the new French Interior Legion, and already he was bored with the farm and quiet. It was like him to go careening off on his motorcycle before his chest was fully healed, and to consider the almost certain accident as only a joke and a chance for another conquest.

Summers was gone when Leif came out. He glanced at the shed, saw that Rex was still chained securely, and headed for the garage. It took time to put on skid chains and check the car against any possible trouble from the slippery road. But while he realized that Lee wouldn't have bothered, his own habits of caution were too deeply ingrained. He'd stayed at home to run the farm and build up the greenhouses and orchard, planning each step and going slowly. Maybe the full cellar, silo, and fodder bins justified it, but there were times when letters came from Lee, or on Lee's rare visits, when Leif wondered. Just about the only excitement he'd known was from vicarious adventures presented on his TV screen. And as for romance— well, maybe it was all to the good that nothing had ever come of his few affairs.

He could no more dislike his brother than anyone else could, but Leif still felt a trace of resentment whenever he remembered having to give up his studies in science at college because Lee had gone off adventuring.

Then Leif's thoughts veered back to the present, and he began worrying again. Now he wouldn't be able to attend the action meeting, and there would be no one there to present his side of the affair. Summers would never buck the would-be vigilantes who were set to kill Rex. Lee would pick a time like this for trouble.

The wind was increasing in strength, and the dull gray sky was hidden by heavier snow. It was crystalline and sharp, though, bouncing on the frozen mud of the road and whipping against the windshield, still too fine to stick. Leif hunched over the wheel, staring ahead. He turned the heater control to maximum, but the wind whipped out the warmth before he could feel it. Driving back would be rugged.

To make it worse, there were still quite a few cars on the road, and many of them were obviously unused to winter driving on gravel. They were probably city fools, out trying to buy food in the country, and now scared back homeward by the storm. Hoarding and increasingly wild prices were making marketing tough in the cities, and there were still a few farmers—moved by stupidity or cupidity—who were willing to sell what they themselves might need very soon.

He came to a rough stretch of road, hardly more than a one-way lane, then jammed on his brakes as headlights broke around a corner and glared into his eyes. The car skidded and slewed around, but he fought it to the side, almost into the ditch. A big Cadillac swept by him, piled high with foodstuff that could never be kept in any city house. It bounced and skidded on the rutted road but dashed past without slowing.

Leif muttered curses and shifted into low. His foot was just easing up on the clutch when a rap sounded on the right front window. There had been no sight of anyone near before the lights of the other car blinded him. But as he hesitated, the rap came again.

He swung his head, expecting to see only a broken branch from a near-by tree. His eyes stared into a red-bearded face and a pair of dark eyes, set too narrow and too deep. It was a handsome face, from what the beard revealed, but something in it made Leif draw back before he caught himself and unlocked the door. The feeling of shock increased as the man climbed in; then the feeling died abruptly.

"Thanks. They call me Laufeyson," the stranger announced coolly. There was a hint of a chuckle in his voice, and his lips parted in a fleeting smile that held a queerly sardonic twist. "I'll ride with you, Leif Svensen, since you're going my way. I'm happier not to walk, with the Fimbulwinter already upon us."

The word struck a familiar chord, and Leif groped for it, forgetting his fleeting puzzle over Laufeyson's knowing his name and the man's sudden appearance. Then the word came back, dredged from the stories he'd heard as a child from his grandmother. "The Fimbulwinter—the dreadful winter. Wasn't that supposed to come before the Twilight of the Gods, or some such?"

"Twilight—or night?" For a moment, Laufeyson's shadowed eyes were cold. Then the wrinkles around them deepened in a deliberate amusement as the stranger studied Leif. "The old blood runs strong in you, Leif Svensen, if you remember that the Fimbulwinter comes before the Ragnarok. As I already knew by your looks. Eh, it darkens early. You're lucky for the lights in this—this car."

Leif nodded, staring out at the weather. Fimbulwinter! The name fitted. Tattered shreds of the old Norse legends came back to him from his grandmother's tales. It was the winter before the gods were to fight their hopeless, fatal battle with the giants. The grimness of the legends had always depressed him, and now the setting was all too suitable in mood. He reached for the radio, to turn on a local FM station that would carry the weather reports and news. Beside him, the stranger jumped at the sound of the voice from the speaker, his red beard seeming to bristle suddenly. Then he chuckled and sat back to listen.

The news was hardly less grim than the tales of Ragnarok. Even the southern hemisphere was in the grip of savage storms, and the seemingly impossible war between Australia and New Zealand was settling into a long and savage affair. There were food riots in the east, crime everywhere, fanatic groups in California, a third war beginning in South America, and utter chaos in China and India. The Muslim faith was sweeping over Russia, and there was dark muttering of a new jihad. So far, the United States had kept out of all these petty wars, but insane pressures were building up.

In nearby Brookville, the Olson brothers had quarreled and killed each other with kitchen knives over who should carry in the wood. Hate groups and vigilantes were meeting regularly, and city hoodlums were forming gangs to invade the surrounding country. Guns and ammunition were being advertised openly on the radio. And there were three more accounts of the angel riders in the sky, with some nonsense about their avoiding the air over churches. Finally, the announcer began on the weather, his voice taking on a forced optimism as he tried to make it sound like something besides a reading of doom.

Laufeyson broke in on that. "Your Norns in the box make no sense," he said. "Why talk of wind direction, when every fool knows that the winds blow from all quarters at Fimbuljahr? And who needs such a voice to know what must come? Unless I smell it wrong, there'll be three days of blizzard, with snow above the head of a tall man."

Leif grunted disgustedly and cut off the radio; Laufeyson might be as accurate as the forecasts being given out now, at that. He slowed as he came to another side road.

"Far as I go in this direction."

"I'll go on with you, Leif, until you find your brother. I'm seeking a meeting and a wolf—though not as the One-Eyed thought—and Faulkner's steading is as near as any for me."

Leif stole a quick glance at him, but something about the expression of the hitchhiker held back his curiosity. He shrugged off a shiver that ran up his spine and concentrated on his driving over the pitted little road. Faulkner's small, weather-beaten house came into view. Lee's motorcycle was in front, crumpled badly, and already being covered by snow. Only the luck of a fool could have saved the rider serious injury.

Leif drove up the lane and parked to the lee of the house. "Coming in with me?"

"I'll wait here, now that the wind no longer blows through the car. And when I'm warmer, I'll be on my way." Leif let it go at that, and went up the crackling, snow-covered steps. He knocked, waited, and knocked more loudly, not surprised at the delay, even though his own efforts to date Gail Faulkner two years ago had been futile. When she finally opened the door, there was a flush of red on her face, and she avoided Leif's look. Behind her, Lee Svensen seemed generally pleased with the world, though the knees were ripped from both legs of his pants, and one hand was bandaged.

"Come in and shut the door, son," he advised. "Hot coffee on the stove. You run and fix it, honey. Black, no sugar. Leif probably wants to bawl me out."

Leif grinned wryly, in spite of his irritation. Nobody had ever succeeded in staying mad at Lee, and he was still a sucker for his twin. The expression on their faces was the only dissimilarity in their looks, but it set them completely apart. The unconscious resentment of Lee's too-ready success with girls was already fading as Leif dropped into a chair near the floor radiator, soaking up the heat gratefully.

"Go out and tell Laufeyson—the man out in the car—to come in for some of the coffee, and we'll forget the lecture, Lee. I'm used to your raising hell with my plans."

Lee groaned as he got to his feet, but his steps were lithe and normal as he went out. A moment later, he was back. "Nobody there. Unless you count the biggest hawk I ever saw flying over. What's the joke?"

Leaf got up reluctantly and moved outside. There was no trace of Laufeyson—nor were there any footprints to show how he'd left through the snow. Leif could see where his own footprints led to the house, but there were no others. He started to bend down for closer study, just as a shrill scream pierced the air. Lee was looking up, and Leif followed his gaze. Far above, something moved through the gloom and the thin snow; it might have been a huge hawk, but it was impossible to see clearly enough to be sure. However, several hunters had brought back rumors of such a bird near here recently. The scream came again as the bird streaked off toward the distant village and vanished in the distance. Leif bent down for further inspection of the area around the car, dismissing the hawk from his thoughts.

"Laufeyson must have had his tracks covered by a chance gust of snow," he decided. "I suppose it doesn't matter, but..."

"He probably sprouted wings and flew away as a hawk," Lee said. "And even if he did, so what? Let's get that coffee before we turn into snowmen and freeze solid here."

Leif went in reluctantly, still bothered by the effect Laufeyson had worked on him. Hell, in another month at this rate he'd be seeing whole companies of angels riding through the sky. The whole business wasn't worth worrying about.

He was still worrying it over an hour later, however, while Lee and Gail were laughing together at the other side of the room. Then he heard the sound of a car outside, and Gail's laughter cut off suddenly. She got up quickly and moved toward the kitchen, just as the door there banged loudly. There was a mutter of voices, and then the older Faulkner's voice rising in excitement..."Never seen him before. Some new guy. He got there just when the meeting was breaking up with nothing resolved. You shoulda been there to hear him. Sure put some gumption into Summers and the rest of the weak-kneed bunch. After he got done talking, we all voted for action. Svensen either gets rid of that killer of his, by golly, or we're going to do it ourselves. We're going to get things straight around here..."

Gail had obviously been trying to quiet him, but his words went on until he reached the living room and spotted Leif and Lee. For a second, a sullen embarrassment covered his grizzled face, to match the scarlet and miserable look of his daughter. Then his stooped shoulders squared belligerently.

"You! Get out! Get out of my house, the both of you, before I throw you out. I won't have a Svensen sneaking around here..."

Lee had gotten to his feet and was buttoning his jacket leisurely. There was a thin, savage grin on his lips as he faced Faulkner, and the older man's whipped-up rage seemed to drain away as he faced it.

"We're going, Faulkner. But if you really feel like losing that temper of yours, come on out with me and let it rip. No? Okay, Leif, let's go. Gail honey, I'll be seeing you later. And thanks for the coffee."

The girl stared at her father for a moment, then came forward to open the door for them. Faulkner bellowed an objection and reached for her, but she avoided his grasp. He stood looking at his own hand, unbelievingly, more hurt than angry. Finally, as he had always done when his wife was still alive, he sighed thickly and went clumping up the stairs in defeat.

Gail came out on the porch, starting to apologize. Lee cut her words off, pulling her face up to his. She came up to meet him hungrily—and jerked back with a sudden low scream.

They turned their faces up to follow her frozen gaze.

The sky was black already and the thickening snow was visible only where the lights from the open door and the windows streamed outward. But something white was coming through the air, squarely in the path of that light. A lusty alto voice hit their ears, and a young blonde woman with the build of an Amazon appeared, mounted on the biggest white horse Leif had ever seen. She seemed to be riding down the light, staring straight at the Svensen twins. The horse dropped until its hoofs were beating the air only four feet off the ground. Then her voice lifted in pitch and the horse reared, leaping upward over the porch. The drumming thud of hoofs and her song drifted out into silence.

When they reached the rear of the house, she was gone.

CHAPTER II

Leif Svensen sat in the car, trying to warm it up, while he waited for Lee to make his good-byes to Gail Faulkner. He was trying to understand what he had seen, and wasn't having too much success. The hair on the back of his neck had risen, as in fear, but there had been nothing terrifying about the rider, and he couldn't be sure now whether he had been afraid or not. He could remember now that Lee had seemed more startled than he had been. His brother had taken only a single glance and then had jerked back into the doorway, not emerging until the rider was gone.

As best Leif could remember, the woman had seemed fully human, and the horse might have been a normal stallion; perhaps even its size had been exaggerated by the lighting. It had been too plain for hallucination, and Leif didn't question his sight. Somehow, there were horses that could fly without wings—or there were scientific developments that permitted the projection of such a vision. Either Einstein's work with gravity was finally paying off, or someone had found the secret of television in three dimensions, color, and sound—without a receiver.

But the purpose of using either development here, so far from any center of importance, eluded him.

"Valkyries." Lee's voice broke in on his thoughts as the other twin slid into the car. "Or that's what our ancestors would have called them. I wonder who drew this one to us?" Leif glanced at him sharply as the car began bumping down the lane. For once, Lee's face was serious. "You don't believe in that old legend, do you?"

"I don't know, son. I've seen riders before—and one of them close—much too close for comfort." Lee Svensen grimaced, and his fingers fumbled with the cigarette he was lighting. "In France."

"You didn't say anything about it when you came back."

"I knew you'd never believe it. A lot of things happen in war that don't make good telling."

Lee mashed out the cigarette suddenly. Then he shrugged. "This happened the last day—the day I got the stuff in my chest. We were in an advance unit. I had a lot of new men in my outfit, and we'd had our rear cut off. Logistics were all loused up. Ammunition was getting scarce. So when de Nal and Jordsson—a queer couple of men from the last replacement group—when they came back from foraging to report what looked like an ammo dump, I took them and a couple others in a truck to try a surprise raid on it.

"It wasn't a surprise. The minute we stopped the truck, the other guys opened up on us with a bomb lobber. They got the truck on the first try, but I dropped in time. And that's when I heard a woman kiyoodling overhead. It might have been the same one. Anyway, she was coming down hell-bent for election, yelling her head off, and all set to grab me. That's when the second bomb hit."

He shivered. "I felt something hit me, and I also felt her hand grab at my hair. She was making another grab, when something happened. Time gets all mixed up. I don't know. Anyhow, either the blast picked me up or de Nal knocked me sideways, onto the steps of a church I hadn't even noticed before. The woman rider gave a scream—hasty-sounding, this time—and came to a dead stop ten feet up. TT16111 blacked out."

"And you think being on consecrated ground saved you?" Leif asked. It was all a piece with the silly rumors he'd sneered at, but the fact that his brother was telling it made a difference somehow.

Lee shook his head. "I don't know, I tell you. The priest who dragged me in and hid me until our side came through believed it. He claimed that the decay of religion was loosing the old demons, and that he was convinced these were Valkyries. Me, I'd rather not think about them at all. I—damn it, Leif, I just don't like having one of them follow me here and stare that way."

They drove on silently, each busy with his thoughts, until they reached Five Corners. Leif's eyes were on the road, and he was only vaguely aware of someone standing and waving at the Corners. It was Lee's surprised shout that brought his foot down on the brake, almost too quickly. The car skidded violently, and he fought for control until it finally came to a stop a hundred feet farther on.

Lee was staring back at the figure now heading for them. "De Nal! Leif, that's the guy I told you about. In France." And now Leif could make out the face. "Laufeyson!"

The door of the car was jerked open, and the man slid onto the seat beside Lee. He was chuckling as he slammed the door shut again. "Under any name, it's still easier not to walk in the Fimbul winter, Leif. I'll return with you. Greetings, Lee Svensen. I've come a long way to join you again."

"How'd you find me?" Lee asked. "And why? Recruiting?" The man laughed, as if at a joke too deep to share. "Not for the Legion, Lee Svensen. No. Jordsson and I played dead after the bomb and then—we deserted, you might say. And here I am, while Jordsson is delayed, but joins us later. Or do you give us welcome?"

Leif had his own questions. The whole business with Laufeyson—or de Nal—made no sense. But driving was taking up his whole attention. The earlier crystals of snow had grown larger and wetter, and the windshield wipers were fighting a losing battle. He was forced at times to lift his foot from the accelerator to let a stronger vacuum work them. The blizzard was close at hand, obviously. The wind was rising, and snow was piling up. The ice that had been on the road was treacherous now, with the damper snow like oil on its surface. Even with the yellow fog light, visibility was bad, and he was forced to a slow crawl—or as close as he dared come without loss of traction.

Lee motioned questioningly toward the wheel, but Leif never felt happy when his brother was driving, even under ideal conditions. He went on, judging as much by the feel of the ruts under the car as by what he could see.

At that, he almost overshot his own entrance, until he heard the deep bass barking of Rex. Then he swung in, hunting for the road. He was starting up it when the dog leaped toward them in the glare of the lights.

Lee swore sharply. "I thought you said that Rex was chained."

"He was. Here, boy!" Leif reached over to open the door, but the dog growled uncertainly, the hair rising on his hackles, and sidled away. Laufeyson made a soft noise, and the dog lifted his head and gave vent to a long, uncertain bay.

"Your Rex doesn't like me," Laufeyson said. "There are times when the dogs don't, and the smell is still fresh on me. Let me move back, and bring him in, before we all freeze." With the man in the back seat, the dog crawled reluctantly in with Lee, and Leif drove up the long driveway. "You might look at his collar," he suggested to Lee.

"That's what I am looking at. The chain has been smashed, as if someone took a sledgehammer to it. No, darn it…the links are half mashed, half fused. You'd think a bolt of lightning had hit it. Here."

Laufeyson reached over. The dog growled, then suddenly quieted at a strange phrase in some foreign tongue. Laufeyson caught the end of the chain and held it where Leif could snatch a glance at it. The description Lee had given was correct. It did look odd. With the neighbors cussin' mad about Rex already, it would mean trouble if someone had seen him loose—and there was no way of knowing how long the dog had been free. He wondered who had done it, but there was no way of telling.

The automatic door of the garage had frozen shut, and Lee had to work it by hand. Then they were out, and into the warmth and brightness of the house, Leif leading Rex in and Laufeyson entering coolly behind them. The man glanced about curiously, and the wrinkles around his eyes deepened.

"Better than spending ages tied over three rocks," he said, dropping into a comfortable chair. For a moment, he reminded Leif of a great cat resting in self-satisfied comfort.

Lee had brought down the whiskey and was pouring a shot apiece. Laufeyson seemed to brace himself, but he downed his shot and his grimace was contented. When Leif came back with coffee, the stranger gave it a disgusted look and refilled his glass with the whiskey.

Unconsciously, Leif pulled the nervous dog closer to him, rubbing the great, wolf-like head. "At least, if the storm keeps up, the fools will have time to cool down. Wish I'd been able to reach the meeting."

"The storm will let up for an hour or so, shortly," Laufeyson stated.

Five minutes later, the wind died down, and the outer air turned crisper and colder, but the snow stopped falling. Leif cast another doubtful glance at the red-bearded man, but he was holding his thoughts in careful abeyance. So much in one day needed time for digestion. Besides, there was something about the stranger that seemed to quiet questions before they could be asked.

Leif was pouring himself a second coffee when the phone rang, startling Laufeyson out of his relaxation. The man caught himself and settled back again, staring thoughtfully as Leif answered the phone.

There was an attempt to disguise the voice at the other end, but it was obviously that of Summers. "Svensen? Just a friendly warning. The men are getting together...

"You mean they're out to get Rex, Summers?"

The disguise dropped. "Yeah, that's right, Leif. Now I don't want you to go blabbing I tipped you off, hear? But I'd sure hate to have anything happen to you. So a word to the wise, I say. There's been another killing, over at Engel's. And this time there ain't no mistaking them big dog tracks. I figure it's better if you take care of things first, before..."

Leif hung up, swearing. But before he could get back to his seat, the phone rang again. He growled into it, expecting Summers again. But this time it was a girl's voice. He listened, then turned to Lee. "It's Gail. She wants you." He handed the instrument over, and saw Lee's initial smile turn sour.

"Yeah, honey." Lee held the receiver away from his ear, waiting for her to calm down. "Yeah...Uhm-hmmm...Okay, we'll take care of it. Don't you worry. No, I know you couldn't do anything. You're a sweet kid to call. Sure, honey. Sure. I'll see you soon."

He was frowning as he faced Leif. "It looks lousy for us, son. Gail says the vigilantes met over at her place, and they're out for blood now—from Rex or from us, and they seem to want both. Drat it, Rex couldn't have gotten to Engel's place and back, but we can't prove it. Damn these crazy fools—a little fear of hunger, and they go nuts. I suppose they'll be here in half an hour."

Leif glanced at the clock, realizing for the first time how late it had become. He hadn't even fed the livestock.

It took fifteen minutes, and some of his gloom lifted during the routine work. There was hay and fodder enough in storage for two years, if necessary, and the cattle and pigs wouldn't suffer. Maybe that was at the root of his trouble. Few of the farmers around could face the prospect of the long months ahead without worry, and they must be fermenting envy into hate now.

He went back inside to find Lee tearing busily into closets, holding the hunting rifle in one hand. "Where do you keep the cartridges for this?"

"You used the last on that hunting trip. I ordered more, but Sears hasn't delivered yet."

Lee grinned savagely and tossed the gun aside, to pound up the stairs. He was back with an automatic and several clips. He threw the gun to Leif.

"You take this. At least you know how to use it. I'll get an axe. How about you, de Nal? You with us? Maybe we can out-bluff them, but..." There was no question between Lee and Leif as to what must be done. Rex had been in the family since Lee had brought him back from Alaska as a pup; he belonged, and nobody was going to get him.

Laufeyson came to his feet gracefully, suddenly looking larger than he had before. "I'm not unfamiliar with an axe, if you have a double-bitted one, Lee."

A minute later, he was swinging it about, testing the balance in the close quarters of the woodshed. Overhead, there was a dull thunder of hoofs and a sound of singing. The red-beard looked up, grinned at Lee's startled reaction, and made another graceful practice swing. "They gather for the feasting. And one is yet to come."

One did come, almost on his words. There was a deep bellow from outside, followed by an answering cry from Laufeyson. The door of the shed flew open suddenly, bouncing on its hinges, and a huge bear of a man was through it before it had closed on the rebound. His face was humorless, broad, and stronger than any face Leif had seen. The eyes were dark and seemed to flash in the light of the overhead bulb, while his black beard jutted from his chin like a flag. There was a feeling of massive power about him that seemed almost a solid aura. In one hand, he carried a black, short-handled maul that must have weighed fifteen pounds but seemed like a toy in the leather-gloved fist.

"Jordsson," Laufeyson told Leif. "And a handy man in a fight, though he may bore you betimes with the telling of his deeds."

The maul flashed up warningly, but the man was apparently used to Laufeyson's needling, even though he obviously could not share in the humor of it. His voice was a deep rumble of power. "The nidderlings come, and Nikarr has the shield maids out. The raven master grows impatient."

"And you grow wordy, as I feared. More, and all will be revealed before the time." Laufeyson's voice had a sharp edge to it.

Leif stared at Lee, and saw the same doubt in his brother's look. Something stirred in the back of his mind, trying to make sense out of the words.

But there was no time for further thought; from down the lane, there came the sound of a number of cars. From the grinding of gears and racing of motors, one or more must have gotten stuck. There was the slamming of doors and the cries of men. Then faintly they could hear a body of men coming on foot, with spots of lights showing where lanterns and flashlights were being used.

CHAPTER III

Leif followed the others toward the front of the house, feeling a tightening run through him. His hands were beginning to sweat, and his stomach felt sick. It was one thing to realize the mob was out, but another to hear it on his own land.

Lee snapped on the porch lights. "Shows them up and helps blind them when they try to see us," he said. "It wouldn't work against trained troops with guns, but these men won't like being seen clearly—I hope. How do you feel, son?"

Leif Svensen managed to grin, but his heart wasn't in it. These three professional fighters might think this a small business, but he didn't like the idea of an attempted lynching by his neighbors. A week ago, he'd have laughed at the idea, but now he was almost sure it amounted to that. He could feel the sweat gathering under his armpits, and his legs seemed to melt under him. He glanced at his hands and noticed that they were trembling.

Lee tapped him on the shoulders. "Forget it. You're not going through anything I didn't feel. These affairs take plenty of experience, son. You hang back until you get the drift. Hell, a mob can't shoot straight anyhow. And maybe we can out-bluff them."

Leif muttered unhappily. Sure, he could hang back, with two strangers and a brother just over a wound doing the fighting for him. He could let them take the brunt of it, while he was the man the crowd was after. But he couldn't live with himself afterward. It was all muddled inside him, so mixed up that he wasn't sure whether he was a coward or not. Well, he'd envied Lee his casual adventurousness. Now he'd find whether he liked such things or not. But already he knew that he didn't.

The mob was near now. Most of them drew into a knot just out of the range of brightness from the porch lights, but a few came ahead purposefully. Leif saw Laufeyson slipping toward a shadowed area, but his eyes were pulled back to the group by a yell that seemed to be in Faulkner's voice—the only recognizable thing about the mob, since all wore kerchiefs over their faces or pillow slips with holes chopped out for their eyes. Inside the house Rex began barking wildly, and the sound touched off the men, who came stamping forward.

Lee had the useless rifle conspicuously across one arm as he stepped lithely forward. His voice had a sudden ring of command that must have been learned in a dozen mercenary armies. "Halt! Stand where you are or we'll drill you!"

There was a muttering while they whipped themselves up. Then a man in front took a step forward. "Give us that damned dog and pay for damage, Leif Svensen. This is your last chance."

"Come and take him," Lee suggested. "Bring on your whole mob. You've got thirty skulking back there. Bring them up. Maybe we'll send ten of you back to your wives alive—if you've got enough liquor in you to face an expert marksman."

He began walking forward, one slow, steady step after the other. The men hesitated as he came toward them, and a couple fell back a few steps. Even the leader was wavering. But at the wrong moment, there was an interruption.

Laufeyson stepped from the shadows, holding firmly onto Rex; he must have gone around to the back of the house to collect the dog. The eyes of the wavering mob suddenly left Lee to stare at the animal.

Leif felt sick at the obviously rotten timing. He moved toward the dog, just as the crowd seemed to forget the animal and concentrate on the figure of Laufeyson.

There was a furious, startled shout. "Hey! It's him! The new guy! The dirty stinking traitor's gone over to their side!"

Now Lee was swinging back, his face shocked and furious at Laufeyson's actions. But Laufeyson had eyes only for the group. He stepped farther forward and began calling out names—Summers, Faulkner, Sheriff Collins, and all the rest. Even as Leif realized that nothing could infuriate the mob more than having their disguise pierced, someone let out a yell, and they began boiling forward.

"Ho!" The roar from Jordsson was filled with a sudden savage pleasure. "Ho!" He moved forward, covering Lee while the twin dropped the useless rifle and darted back for his axe.

Jordsson's voice rang out again, like a clap of thunder, and the maul left his hand in an air-piercing sweep. Something splattered out on the snow, and the maul seemed to rebound as if it had hit a spring instead of a head. It bounced back squarely into Jordsson's waiting hand. Leif noticed it abstractly, but his eyes stayed riveted to the headless thing on the ground. The automatic fell from his hands. His stomach heaved, but his throat was too constricted to cooperate.

The crowd flinched, and a few in front leaped back, but the pressure of those behind was too great. Now that blood had been spilled, they reacted like sharks gathering at the smell of death. With a strange, animal sound of sheer fury, they charged forward. Lee, Jordsson, and Laufeyson were moving to meet them, in spite of the guns that were appearing now in all hands. Beside them, Rex was flying through the air in a leap toward an unprotected throat.

Leif bent to recover the automatic, and something whistled by his ear. Realization finally penetrated that it was a bullet. He stood there, stupidly drying the automatic and shoving it into his pocket aimlessly for another minute. Then belated instinct seemed to take over, and he dashed frantically after the other three, who had already driven into the crowd at quarters too close for the firing of guns.

In front of Leif a man was clubbing at Laufeyson s head with a rifle. Lee's axe swept around, leaving a gory trail, and Leif grabbed at the rifle and got it before it could drop from the falling man's hand.

There were axes and knives in the crowd, too. Even as the barrel of the gun fitted into Leif's hand, he was forced to drop the weapon and to grab desperately at the handle of an axe that was being swung at him. It grazed his arm, shredding off leather from his coat, and he was down on the ground, grappling with the axeman and being trampled.

Something reared over him, and a blade chopped expertly down. The hand at Leif's throat went limp, and the axe came free in his grip, just as Laufeyson grabbed his hand and yanked him upright. Whatever the actions of Laufeyson before, there was no question of his loyalty in the battle.

A part of Leif's mind was still wondering automatically whether he was a coward, and another detached fragment was fighting at the sickness he could still feel all through him. But the hysteria of the mob and the ferocity of these former friends and neighbors had entered into him. He swung out underhanded, feeling the axe cut through the leg of someone before him, and moved up beside Laufeyson, who was now separated from the other two.

He still couldn't bring himself to kill deliberately, but maiming and crippling seemed almost as effective. Things became a red haze in front of him for the next few minutes. When it cleared, he could see that most of the attackers were retreating wildly. They had counted on a lynching with little danger, had been swept into something more violent, and were now losing their frenzy in the face of the danger to their lives.

Then Leif heard singing coming from the air above, and he caught a faint glimpse of at least half a dozen of the women on horses, high up and dimly white as they circled against the black of the sky. Then he dropped his eyes.

Jordsson was farthest away, taking a final toll of the retreating mob. Nearer, Rex was dragging himself along by his front legs, obviously wounded. Leif started toward him, then stopped when he saw his brother.

Lee was trying to sit up, holding onto his abdomen where blood was spilling out over the snow from a great, ugly gash. As Leif moved toward him, Lee lifted himself to an elbow, trying to point, and let out a warning cry. But it was too late.

There was a sound behind Leif, and something struck sharply against his back, sending him twisting and reeling. He could see that one of the men who had seemed unconscious was now up and charging toward him. He tried to swing himself around and bring up his axe, but the man had already raised a big corn knife for another stroke. It swished in the air and began chopping down.

Leif jerked sideways, trying to throw himself out of the way. But there was no time. The blade came down remorselessly. It whistled by his ear, hit against his jacket, and went on through. Pain lanced through him as muscles parted and the collar-bone splintered. He was falling now, the big machete-like knife coming loose. He started to shout, but his voice was a burble, and there was the salt of blood in his mouth.

He twisted as he fell. The attacker was coming forward again. Then an axe-bit was buried in the man's skull, and Laufeyson was kicking the falling corpse aside. Laufeyson sank to his knees, lifting Leif's head in one arm, while Leif made waving motions and opened his mouth in a wild shout toward the sky. Laufeyson's arm was gentle, but his lips were smiling in triumph as he looked at Leif Svensen!

Wild singing was coming from the air above, and with it came the thunder of hoofs, beating like a muffled drum. An object flashed down as the pain in Leif began to sharpen and become unbearable. It separated into a big woman on an immense horse, dropping out of nowhere. Everything was turning into a gray mist, but consciousness had not left entirely. He felt her hands clutch his hair, felt himself lifted with a single heave of her arm and dropped across the shoulders of the horse.

Then the wind was whistling about him, and he could sense the earth falling away. Behind him, the song suddenly rose to a strange shrieking set of tones, and they seemed to twist crazily. Rainbow spots merged into great bands and seemed to quiver through Leif's whole body, blotting out the pain.

The horse was laboring now. Its breath came in short, hard gulps, and the huge hoofs seemed to slip and slide. Again, the rider urged her mount onward, while the rainbow bands quivered, tightened, and relaxed. Leif felt the sweat from the horse begin to soak into him, stinging sharply as it worked into his wound, lifting the pain to new heights.

Again the horse strained, and something seemed to give with sticky reluctance. The pattern of the rainbow ran together, beating almost audibly. The horse seemed to breast some sort of a rise, and his hoofs settled again into the steady pounding, while the woman's shout turned back to the song she had first been singing.

There were words and names in the song that seemed familiar. Even the language tugged at his memories, reminding him of words and names his grandmother had used. It was as if the pain were driving his mind back to its beginnings. Warrior maids—the shield maidens—who rode through the air over some magical bridge named Bifrost. A brawling, stalwart super-man with 'a hammer who could cause tides by drinking the ocean; a sly one chained to rocks under a serpent's venom; giants and monsters; wonders and a doom that must destroy everything including the earth.

It was a myth and a language dead a thousand years. It was nonsense.

There was a violent wrenching that threatened to tear Leif apart, atom by atom, and the rainbow colors of Bifrost poured out in a wild final burst.

Then all grew quiet. Blackness closed over Leif Svensen mercifully.

CHAPTER IV

The sound of distant metallic clashing and the shouts of men reached Leif's ears, with a realization of the passage of hours in unconsciousness. He stirred, before remembering his wounds. But the pain was gone. Either a lot of time had passed, or the whole final part of the mob battle had been only a delusion from a concussion. Now he was obviously on some sort of a bed, though the usual hospital smell was lacking. There was a subtle feeling of strangeness that told him he was not in his own house, either. He opened his eyes, then blinked them shut. The darkness was the same in either case, though he could feel no bandages across his face to shut out the light.

From nearby, he heard a sudden stirring and the sound of footsteps. He lay quietly, afraid to move yet and find how badly he was hurt, wondering why the lights were out.

"The trance still lasts," a woman's soft voice said. A hand ran across his forehead caressingly, and he could feel the hair being pushed back from his face. The fingers remained another moment, and there was a welcome coolness and an odd tingle to the touch. "He's slim for a hero, as Balder was —and comely, too. But I find no war lines on his face. He looks—perhaps gentle…

There was a lusty answering laugh, heavy with amusement. "Be careful, Fulla. Such words are odd in a virgin of the Asynjur. Remember Freyja's mortal husband."

"You go too far, Reginleif." There was confusion in the voice of the girl called Fulla. "Though it has been a long time since a mortal joined us. And the Aesir grow empty as the einherjar. Oh, nonsense!"

The other laughed again, but did not press the point. "He was trouble enough. Carrying him through Bifrost was almost too much for even the loan of Gna's favorite Hoof-Tosser. The horse will be good for nothing for a week now. And I'm still weak and worn from holding your hero to the horse. Let's hope this man is a real berserker, with the knowledge the Sly One tells Asa-Odin we need. Surtr's hot breath is getting too close."

There were retreating footsteps, and the voices faded. Leif Svensen lay frozen, turning the fresh madness over in his head. Balder, Aesir, Odin— the gods of the ancient Norse. This must be more of his delirium. Yet there had been the Valkyr ride—and the hammer that returned to Jordsson, like the ancient hammer of Thor. It was ridiculous.

And where was Lee? He struggled to a sitting position. "Lee!"

He had heard no sound, but a hand touched his shoulder, pushing him back with a strength that must be that of a man. "Quiet, Leif Svensen. Your brother will be cared for. I could wish—but no matter. Bifrost has burned your sight. Here, take my hand and make your eyes follow the feel of its motions." Laufeyson's voice held no amusement now, but seemed worried. "You'll need all your senses at the Thing. I've some skill at sleight, as has been told. If you've guessed who I am by now, remember that. Now…"

The motions were a curious hocus-pocus, and the next words came as a chant:

> *By Ironwood's mother,*
> *This matter make right;*
> *Speed minutes; and man,*
> *Still mortal, gain sight!*

It worked. The room sprang into sudden light. Leif blinked, looking at the aged beams of the ceiling. The room was huge, with hard wooden bunks around it, covered with bearskins. Weapons of primitive design decorated the walls, and the light streamed in from tiny windows of oiled parchment. It was no hospital, but something from the scenes of a second-rate production of a Wagnerian opera. Leif's eyes jerked to his shoulder. There were no bandages or open wounds, but only a livid red scar to mark where the wound had been.

He swung to the one he had known as Laufeyson, who was now wearing a helmet with spikes and wings and was clad in heavy mail "Loki! And this…"

Loki nodded. "I'm Loki Laufeyson, and also the son of Nal. And this is Asgard—the home of your ancestors' gods. You're whole, Leif, though you had to be near death before you could be ripped from your ties to Earth. Going through the dimensional bridge of Bifrost revitalizes the body until it can repair such damage in a day. And yes, you're looking at myths—but myths with sharp teeth, Leif Svensen. To convince you—what language am I speaking?"

Leif could remember the English words for *myth* and *dimensional* in the speech, but the rest—he couldn't place the words, though they seemed clear in his mind. It was like his grandmother's language, but incredibly changed—or incredibly older.

"We can't read minds here," Loki explained. "But any vocalized words carry their meanings to all—such is the nature of Asgard. Each of the worlds we know has its own peculiar laws. Will you believe?"

Leif shook his head, still uncertain. Something was wrong, but he couldn't turn off his scientific training to accept the other's words so quickly. Neither could he wholly deny them, particularly from the fragmentary hints of reason that Loki's words had offered.

Loki frowned. "No matter—you'll have to believe. Already Fulla returns. Listen, then, and remember! Play dead, as you were, as long as you can. And follow my lead later. Valfather Odin is stubborn—and sometimes a fool. After I was recalled and convinced him a modem man was needed, he chose Lee. Thor and I were sent for him, but I connived things in such a way that I could take you instead. But we can both suffer for the deceit. To the others, you must be the berserker, your brother, who could hold back a score in blood-rage to save a friend, as Odin saw from his throne. Remember that, and play the part. And play it well. Odin's rage is not pleasant! "

Steps were sounding from outside, and Loki was suddenly gone. Where he had been, a leaf was drifting on a gentle wind, to blow out through the doorway. Leif stared at it, his head spinning with too much and too little information. Delirium or not, he was sure that this was the time to follow orders. Loki's worry had been genuine, at least. He dropped back quickly, closing his eyes and blanking out all expression. "Still in a trance," Reginleif's rough voice commented.

"It should have been gone by now." Fulla's hand again rested softly on his forehead. "But nothing goes right since the awakening. Even the apples...Perhaps appointing me in Idunn's place was a mistake. The tree responds to nothing I do. Well, he must be revived, Reginleif."

Reginleif tittered hoarsely. "I've revived enough heroes, Fulla, and Hoof-Tosser needs a rubdown. Besides, after that last ride, I don't have energy enough to pass to him. You do it—since you want to, anyhow."

Leif opened his eyes a crack, just enough to see the buxom woman leaving. Fulla was moving across the room toward him hesitantly, slim and supple, her hair long and golden, bound at the back by a curious metal crown of the same color. Her face had the beauty of a type sometimes called sweet or wholesome, when women wanted to be catty about their envy, and the blush that was covering her cheeks now added to the effect. Then she was too close, and Leif closed his eyes quickly.

There was hesitation in her movement as she touched him this time. Her arm moved under his head, while her other hand rested on his chest. And suddenly her lips were on his, full and warm, pressing gradually closer! Something like an electric current seemed to run between them, a warm glow of strange force.

Leif's arm moved automatically around her, pulling her closer and tightening. "No. Ymir, no!" she gasped. "Not under the spell, or there will be a twining!" But his arm was stronger than her resistance, and their lips met again. This time, the warm flux of force seemed to go both ways. For a moment, until it seemed to weaken, she permitted it, her hand even moving to his shoulder and her lips responding. Then her breath caught in a thick gasp, and she jerked back, her face deathly white.

She looked better with his eyes fully open, and he grinned. The white of her face changed to crimson under his gaze.

"It was only customary—to awaken a hero entranced…" She stammered slightly over the words. Then her lips drew to a thin line as she studied him. "But you were revived before! You tricked me!"

The delirium was definitely taking a turn for the better, Leif decided, and the unreality of the situation cut off the last of his inhibitions. Besides, he was under Loki's directions to act as Lee Svensen would. "Sure I tricked you," he admitted cheerfully, catching her hand. "What kind of man wouldn't, if he could?"

She struggled, half-heartedly and with a look of self-surprise. Halfway to him, she gave up all pretense and came to meet him eagerly. His grin vanished, and he was briefly shocked at his own response. There was no flux of fire this time, but something inside him seemed to gather itself together and burst. He was only conscious of Fulla and the need to be nearer her, to gather her more tightly to him…

"Odin summons!" A hoarse croak announced it, followed by the caw of a crow. Fulla sprang back from Leif, the red of her face rushing up and disappearing into the roots of her hair. Leif followed her gaze, to see a black bird sitting on the shoulder of a shaggy grey wolf.

The bird regarded him steadily. "Odin summons the Son of Sven to the Thing. Let Fulla bring him."

It cawed again, beat its wings and was off, with the wolf loping after it.

Fulla avoided Leif's eyes and began pulling a helmet and corselet of mail from the wall. "Put these on quickly. The Alfadur is impatient these days. And—we'll forget this folly."

Her modesty didn't extend to any taboos about nudity, he noticed. He was scrambling into the odd get-up, and she was not only watching but trying to speed things up by helping. He tried to remember the mores of the Norse legends, but nothing about that seemed to come back. He was surprised to find that her attitude didn't bother him. Maybe this was more of the automatic conditioning to Asgard.

He had no intention of forgetting what had happened; nor, he thought, did she. But he followed her out quietly. The building sprawled over acres of ground, low and massive, with door after door in the front. Other buildings lay around it, some higher, but none over four stories. Most had been gilded once, but now only faint flecks of gold caught the sunlight. Asgard seemed badly in need of repairs.

The land itself was much more impressive. The air seemed crystal clear, until it reached up to a layer of solid white cloud, like a uniform layer of infinite depth, but with light still spilling through. In the distance a low range of hills ran off into the horizon. A high wall cut off one side, and a dense forest lay in front. In all other directions he saw that the greensward of rolling plains continued on and on; the grass was soft and springy underfoot. It might have been a well-kept lawn.

They headed for the forest. Then as they moved away from the huge, peeled-log buildings, Leif saw the source of the sounds he had heard on first awaking. There was a plain that occupied many square miles, and most of it had been worn down to the bare dirt. Now it was covered thickly with men in mail, slashing and poking away busily at each other. Some held double-bitted battle axes, others carried spears, and most were equipped with clumsy broadswords and shields.

As he watched, a warrior not fifty feet away swung at two others, lopping off their heads with a single stroke. The warrior wiped his forehead complacently and moved lazily down the field, apparently looking for more trouble. A spear swished through the air, piercing his side. He stopped, staring at it stupidly; then he sat down, not even bothering to remove it.

It looked horrible, but Leif was beginning to remember more of the myths. These would be the einherjar, the heroes that the Valkyries brought here to Valhalla to fight in practice until needed at the Ragnarok. Odin, ruler of this place, made them whole again each evening, so a little head-cutting didn't really matter. Leif noticed that the wounds seemed to produce no blood.

"Your heroes look sluggish," he commented.

Fulla nodded unhappily. "Most are, though these are the greatest of warriors. The white elves' false flesh doesn't hold the vital force well, even though it is caught at the very moment of death."

"*False* flesh?"

"So we call it—or called it—before the way to the world of the elves was closed." She seemed surprised at his ignorance but went on after a moment. "The Valkyries carry a seed of the flesh in their mouths and breathe it into the mouth of a dying hero. Then when it is drawn forth again, it holds the shape and force of the hero until more flesh can be added here to bring back full weight. But we have found no way to stop the loss of force with time."

A matrix of something like the alleged ectoplasm to shape itself to the original cell and memory pattern, Leif decided. Then he grimaced at his effort to make sense out of anything here. "Why not bring back the real hero instead of such stuff?"

She sighed. "Even Bifrost cannot revive the dead. Elf flesh has no true death, and re-forms by itself. As for snatching a mortal before death severs his bond to his world—well, you should know how difficult that is. Even with two of our few apples, Hoof-Tosser could not bring you here without help…Nor can we stand talking any longer. Come."

Leif looked at his body. Apparently it was his, and not some ectoplasmic stuff. It didn't feel at all ethereal as he watched her moving ahead of him. They crossed a stream on rocks and entered the woods through a well-worn path. Then he caught her again, pulling her to him. She responded briefly before drawing away.

"We'll be late," she protested softly. "The Aesir are assembled at Yggdrasil."

They were, as Leif saw a few minutes later. The fabled tree was really a group of ancient ash trees, with tangled branches spreading like a canopy overhead. Odin sat in a hard chair, recognizable by the wolves at his side, the ravens on his shoulders, and the one piercing eye that stared out of an old and glum face at the assembly. For a moment, Leif felt pity at the sight of the bowed shoulders and the doom and frustration on the god's countenance.

Loki was waiting. He smiled and moved toward them.

Fulla made a hasty sign with her fingers and tried to draw Leif aside. "The Evil Companion. The Aesir are mad to let him return. Guard yourself against him, Leif."

Leif Svensen frowned. He was remembering tales of Loki's treachery and troublemaking. Fulla's warning wasn't unfounded, from the old tales. But he had no choice now; Loki was the only one of the council he could count on. "I think Loki is my sponsor," he told her.

She went rigid and her face blanched, as if he had slapped her. Her hand, which had rested on his arm, jerked back and went to her lips. Disgust ran over her face. Without a word, she whirled on her heels and moved away from him.

Loki was beside him at once, chuckling softly. "She doesn't like me, Leif," he said needlessly. "Once when Asgard faced danger, I arranged for a truce with Muspelheim on condition she marry the head giant's son. He had a boar's head and four arms, but he was better than most of them. She got Freyja to bail her out, but she's hated me since. Now she probably feels that you've betrayed her. But enough of that." He drew Leif closer to the assembly, pointing. "I see you recognize Odin. Vidarr and Vali, his sons, are beside him. Watch them—they're supposed to live on after Ragnarok, and I suspect they're plotting to speed it. Then Heimdallr, who'll oppose anything I wish…

He went on, but Leif couldn't keep track of all the gods and their relationships. His head was spinning as he followed Loki toward the throne of Odin.

Odin glowered down at him, while the cold face of Odin's wife, Frigg, refused to see him. Odin motioned, but it was for Fulla. She came up with a chest, and Odin pulled out a small green apple. He nibbled at it, swallowed, and passed it on. The bitterness in his voice might have been from ulcers.

"Phhaa! Are we to gain our youth and strength on such as that?" He belched unhappily. "And not even enough of those. Loki, where is our son Thor?"

"Oku-Thor has not returned. Perhaps he seeks more heroes." Loki's voice was humble and apologetic, but changed to relief as he spoke sideways to Leif. "We're in luck there. I was afraid that Thor would get back too soon. He'd probably recognize that you were only the hero's twin, and have us both cast into Niflheim."

"And the hero?" Odin asked.

Leif followed through the crowd, noticing the stares directed toward his boots and the watch still on his wrist. Loki's voice suavely began the tale of how he and Thor had tried to get their man in battle, to be defeated by hallowed ground. He told of following to another land, and of the difficulty in arousing the neighbors and creating the battle there. Leif noticed a skillful blend of his own part with Lee's. He also sickened as he listened to the duplicity Loki had practiced in stirring up the neighbors and then cold-bloodedly aiding in killing them, just to make sure that Leif would be seriously wounded, and suitable for passage over Bifrost. Apparently, by some tradition, only wounds gained in combat could count. He could almost agree with Fulla's judgment of Loki. But there was nothing he could do now but play along.

Odin listened impatiently until the tale was finished. "Little enough, but I suppose it must do. It's an ill age when men turn to women, and your hero lacks the shoulders even to swing a good axe. Still, if he has the skills they've used to replace their waning courage, we must use him. Loki, do you sponsor this Son of Sven against the Ragnarok?"

Loki lifted his hand. Beside Odin, the thin-faced Vali and the fat Vidarr turned quickly and began muttering. Odin cut them off, his shoulders sagging further.

"What more can we do?" he asked almost querulously. "The times are mad, and we grow mad with them. Even Loki we must trust, since this is a time attuned to him. If this hero of Loki's fails us, we can be no worse off, and you may have the two of them for your sport. Son of Sven, step forward!"

"We're in luck. Odin's had opposition enough to grow stubborn in our favor," Loki began. But a sudden roar stopped him.

"Hold!" The roaring bellow came from the rear, and Loki swore hotly. The huge figure of Jordsson—or Thor—came jostling through the ranks of the assembly. At his heels ran a tired, panting dog that Leif recognized as Rex. In his arms, Thor was carrying the body of Lee!

"Hold!" Thor roared again. He dropped Lee Svensen with surprising gentleness onto the turf and swept his eyes back over the group, searching. Loki had pulled Leif back quickly, losing them in a thicker group. Thor scowled and faced Odin again.

"Father Odin," he announced, "this is the hero, the real Son of Sven. I denounce the other as an impostor, and as great a knave as Loki. I have been betrayed. I demand justice!"

His eyes swung toward the foppish Heimdallr, who stopped polishing his fingernails against his thighs long enough to point to Loki and Leif. Then Thor turned toward them, reaching for the hammer at his side.

CHAPTER V

Odin's voice took on a sharp note of command as he cut through the confusion. "Enough, Thor! This is a judging place, and these matters need thought. How comes this man without a Valkyr to guide him?"

Thor's scowl remained, but his impatient hand dropped slowly, and Loki breathed a sigh of relief as he began dragging Leif cautiously forward. Thor's anger was obviously still hot, but he was trying to control it.

"There were no Valkyries after Loki befuddled them into taking that one." Thor jerked a thumb contemptuously toward Leif Svensen. "Reginleif and the others went off, leaving me with the hero dying at my feet. I carried him through Bifrost on my back. How else?"

"And the dog? Since when is Asgard for beasts?"

"Since ravens and wolves were brought here!" Thor snapped back. Surprisingly, Odin almost smiled at that, but Thor went on without waiting to note the response. "Two of the nidderlings had almost killed the animal before my hammer Mjollnir found them. Yet the stout-hearted beast, dying and with a broken back, still crawled after us. Over half the way he came on his own. Should I have refused him help while Loki's dupe rode on Hoof-Tosser? He came here in my arms, and right welcome to his place!"

There was a clamor at that, and even Loki's face showed sincere admiration. "Even Hoof-Tosser at his best couldn't have carried both," he muttered to Leif. "But when Thor's angry, he'd carry twenty through Bifrost. It will sway the Aesir to his side, though."

Leif had almost given up any effort to think in the chaos of events, but he caught at Loki's shoulder now. "I'm calling it off, Loki. I won't fight against my brother."

"A noble gesture, eh?" Loki grinned. "Don't worry. Thor wouldn't carry Lee here and then desert him. He may not be bright, but he's just, in his own way. Lee Svensen will do well enough, whatever happens. But unless we win this affair, you won't. You *can* be killed, even here, since you're wearing your own flesh instead of elf-shapings. And that's the least worrisome of Odin's dooms."

Now they were near the front of the throng, and Loki raised his hands ceremoniously for attention. Thor scowled at him, but Odin nodded slowly.

"A mighty feat, Thor," Loki began, keeping his voice just low enough that the others had to strain to hear. The trick quieted them. "Bragi will make a new poem of it. But a pity, too, since I'd already sent the real hero on. Alfadur Odin, in the confusion of the fracas, it was easy to confuse the deeds of two who seemed exactly alike. Only by holding myself back, and letting Thor do most of the infighting, was I able to keep them straight."

"What?" Thor's ear-splitting bellow was a fresh shock every time Leif heard it. "You claim I don't know a hero, Loki? Now, by Ymir…"

Loki shrugged. "Not an unconscious one, Oku-Thor. Dying men are all alike. No, I claim only that you were too intent on the battle to see all, as I did in my humbler role. Fulla, you were present when he arrived. Say whether my candidate seemed a coward."

Leif looked at her quickly. But the warmth was still missing from her face, and her voice was cold and disdainful. "How should I know, Father of Evil? He seemed grievously wounded, from the scars that had not gone completely. But a mortal creature who would choose to be with you can hardly be trusted, or even have his wounds known for real, rather than by your sleight."

"And did he cower when he was confronted by a goddess, Fulla?" Loki asked, and the grin was back on his lips. "Even such a one as you, whose virtue is known to be above the will of the needs of Asgard? Or did he perhaps seem eager to try his luck where even gods might fail? Surely you would know of that."

She flushed under Loki's gaze, and her eyes swung to Leif Svensen accusingly. Then she turned away coldly, her chin raised a trifle too high. "He was bold enough—bold enough to be *your* twin!"

She came by Leif then, not a foot away, and it seemed to him that the angle of her head away from him was almost too deliberately calculated. She moved on toward Thor. "Oku-Thor, your hero needs reviving, and since no Valkyr has volunteered, perhaps my help would be welcome."

She made certain small gestures and seemed to be reciting something. Then she dropped to her knees on the turf, lifting Lee's head in her arms. Leif swore—she needn't have made that much of a production of it. Then he cursed himself for thinking it while Lee was in need of help—and swore again as Lee opened his eyes and grabbed for her. Frigg's cold, disapproving cough put an end to that, however, and Fulla stood erect, staring at Leif with a thin, chill smile on her lips.

Lee Svensen shook his head and came to his feet, looking at the group around him. Leif expected shock and surprise, but Lee merely frowned, shook his head, and suddenly laughed.

"I'll be blasted—grandmother's Asgard! Thor, Odin—and Loki de Nal." He shook his head again, staring into the crowd. Then his face cleared. "And Leif! Damn it, son, I'm glad they got you, too, even if it is selfish."

Fulla carefully moved to the other side of Lee as Leif came up, grabbing for his brother's hand. Rex let out a wild bark and was leaping up and down, licking at the faces of the twins indiscriminately. Thor muttered unhappily as the brothers came together, showing their complete similarity. His eyes were doubtful as Loki joined them with a grin on his lips.

The puzzled mutter of the group around reached Leif's ears dimly, but his thoughts were churning busily over the fact that Lee could take everything in at one quick glance and seemingly enjoy what he found. Apparently he could also sweep Fulla to him in less time. But Leif's throat was oddly constricted as he felt the solid grip of his brother. "You look a lot better than the last view I had of you, Lee."

"Two heroes, both alike, both wounded in battle," Loki commented loudly, while Thor regarded him with a mixture of distrust and strange, grudging respect. "Yet it is well known that names have power, too. Should the old blood not be stronger in one named Leif?"

Thor's grunt told Leif that it was a telling stroke; the gods were apparently better at tradition than logic, and name magic had been a considerable part of that tradition. He was trying to fill in the essential facts for Lee, but he stopped to stare at the assembly.

Heimdallr frowned and stopped polishing the metal on his corselet. The god's fatuously self-satisfied look sharpened as he stared at Leif. "Two heroes, Loki? But my eyes, which can see the grass grow at a thousand miles, tell me your hero has one wound only, and that in his back. And I think it is the only battle wound he has known."

Loki's grin slipped for a second, and Leif felt his palms begin to sweat. He began to suspect that Loki's smile was only a mask for worry. The seriousness of all this was slowly dawning on him. He rubbed his hands against his strange garments, bringing them up against something hard in the leather pouch Fulla had buckled onto him. It was the automatic which he must have transferred along with his other few possessions without noticing what he was doing. He reached for it, even as Loki recovered from his brief consternation.

"Heimdallr's eyes see more than rumors this time, then. Of course it was a blow struck at his back—because none dared to face him while the battle rage was on him!"

But Loki's hesitation had been noticed, and the face of Odin was sharpening into determination. Surprisingly, Thor looked uncertain now, still muttering. But the doubts on the expressions of the others were vanishing.

Leif braced himself, having to force himself to the realization that Loki could protect him only to a limited extent. He'd been passive up to now, but it looked as if the only saving of the situation would have to be of his own doing. He jerked out the automatic and pointed it at the smirking face of Heimdallr.

"If..." Leif swallowed, caught his voice, and somehow managed to stiffen himself against a picture of Lee in the same situation. "If you're to blow the horn that gives Asgard notice of Ragnarok, Heimdallr, you'll do it better without a hole in your head! And if the rest of you want that warning, you'd better see he stays in fighting condition. Or haven't you seen what one of these things can do?"

He aimed and pulled the trigger as he finished; the report jerked every god up, like connected puppets rising together. The bullet plowed into a knot on the tree a foot above Heimdallr's head, showering splinters and dust down on the god and washing the smugness off his face at once. Leif was grateful for the target practice he'd kept up, even when Lee was away. "The next goes through Heimdallr!" he warned.

"No!" Thor's hand leaped forward, and the hammer whipped out, barely grazing the automatic. But there must have been magnetism in the metal of the maul. It drew the gun to the hammer and jerked it from Leif's hand, carrying the automatic back to Thor, along with the returning maul.

Thor pulled it free and held it loosely. "A good play, Leif Svensen, but Heimdallr's Gjallar-Horn is needed."

Leif had turned, expecting the big hammer to come at him next, but Thor stood calmly regarding him. Apparently the big god had his own code, and direct action was no violation of it. Heimdallr let out a sudden shout, but quieted at a word from Odin and turned to confer quickly with Vali and Vidarr.

Loki was speaking again. "You wanted proof—and you have it. As was shown from Odin's throne, the heroes now have new weapons, and ones which we need if Surtr's host is to be overcome. Who but a hero would have such, or know so well the use of it? Let Thor's candidate produce such a weapon, if he can!"

"You know damned well I can't," Lee said quietly. "However..."

He had moved closer to Thor. Now his arm chopped down abruptly on Thor's wrist, sending the automatic spinning; his other hand snapped out to catch the gun. Thor blinked, scowled, and gave a sudden booming chuckle of approval at Lee's audacity. The approval broke off sharply as Lee tossed the gun to Leif. With another sudden movement, Lee had a two-bitted axe from a bystander and was moving to cover Leif's back.

"A hero, as all can see," Thor shouted toward Odin.

Loki snorted. "A hero, to be sure—when Thor drops the weapon into his hand! It proves nothing. Can your hero make such weapons for the Aesir, Oku-Thor? We've heroes enough for brawling already in Valhalla. We need ones with skills."

"Is that what we're here for?" Lee asked in a whisper. "Make modern weapons for these anachronisms?"

Leif was careful to hide his lips from Heimdallr. The god might be a popinjay in some ways, but his eyesight was obviously a lot better than average, and his steady stare seemed to indicate that he might be able to read lips. "Seems so. I suppose we could make some kind of a stab at it, if they have any materials here. I remember some of my college chemistry, and I've handled tools enough on the farm. But I'd be lucky to come up with flint-lock carbines and ball shot."

Thor was standing uncertainly, while Odin looked at him expectantly. Finally the black-bearded god turned to Lee. "Can you, Lee Svensen?"

"Of course not," Lee answered. "Using guns and making them are two different things where I come from. Besides, I don't have the materials for it. You might ask my brother."

Odin turned toward Leif, who felt himself beginning to sweat again. He looked toward Loki, but the god was staring at the ground, muttering something, and apparently paying no heed to what was happening. It was up to Leif, it seemed. Well, maybe he could make some kind of weapon, but he had no idea of how long it might take with whatever he could find in Asgard. He was sure that Odin would never accept a promise to deliver weapons in some distant future. There had been too many references to Ragnarok being near. They wanted immediate delivery.

He was bracing himself for an answer when Loki moved in front of him. One hand was behind the god's back, and he moved it suggestively while addressing Odin. "A difficult task, as Lee says, and one which takes material. Fortunately—and at great effort—I brought with me such material, enough for one gun only, and that without ammunition. Leif will now make such a gun for all to see."

CHAPTER VI

The hand moved suggestively behind him again, and Leif looked down this time to see an automatic on the palm! Loki slipped it deftly under his corselet, then turned to face Leif, screening them both from any danger of lip-reading by Heimdallr. "Hide your motions and pretend you're having a bit of difficulty," Loki ordered softly. "And throw your gun to Lee before you do anything else."

Loki picked up one of the crude baskets lying on a bench and began tossing something into it where all could see, drawing the stuff from his pouch. It looked like a collection of rocks. At his nod, Leif threw his automatic to Lee, then took the basket and moved with it to another bench near one of the trees, where no one could see the contents. Loki's automatic had somehow been transferred from Loki's garments to the basket, and now lay on top of a small collection of rubble.

Leif buried his hands in the basket, trying to seem actively busy with the contents. His first idea was to disassemble and then reassemble the gun, but that proved impossible. For some reason the parts refused to come loose as they should. All he got for his pains was a sliver in his finger, probably from the rubble. Finally, he contented himself with going through the motions without touching the gun, trying to time it as if he were really working with a standard automatic. He saw Loki drift over toward Lee and watched Lee's face brighten; some information must have passed. Then the god was back beside him, nodding.

Leif straightened, holding up the second automatic and turning carefully so as to catch his elbow on the basket and send it spinning and scattering what was left in it. Loki grunted in approval. But Leif's eyes were on Thor, who moved forward to study the gun. Finally the black-bearded head nodded reluctantly.

A clamor went up from the crowd, and Odin sagged back into his seat, seemingly still not sure. Heimdallr was trying to gain the ruler's attention, but the noise of the crowd made it impossible. He turned toward Vali and Vidarr and began saying something, his gestures emphatic as Odin lifted his hand for silence.

Vali's voice cut through the noise first. "Father Odin, it would seem that Loki spoke truth this once, and that Leif shall be the man to hold off Ragnarok."

Vidarr leaned over, speaking quickly into the ear of his father, while the crowd set up a fresh roar. Heimdallr sprang to his feet, shouting and pulling at Vali, but the crowd noise covered his words. Finally, Vali caught him, making frantic motions until he sat back again, scowling. Then, as quiet slowly came, Odin turned to Leif.

"We have decided then, Leif, Son of Sven. We distrust your patron still, and we distrust the arts of weakness that have made men lose the art of their own sinews and good steel. But we have no choice other than to try even such skills against the Day that draws so quickly nigh. Prepare the weapons against Ragnarok, and you shall have any one request within our not inconsiderable power to grant. Betray us, or give us cause to doubt, and Niflheim shall claim both you and your patron Loki. By Ymir, we swear it. As for the other…"

"As for the other," Thor's voice broke in heavily, "I have brought Lee Svensen to Asgard under my safe conduct. Does any question the honor of Thor?"

Obviously, nobody did. He scowled from face to face, then nodded. "Lee shall lead the einherjar with me," Thor finished. He started off, motioning for Lee to follow. Surprisingly, Rex got up and trotted along behind him.

"Be seeing you, son," Lee called. He went off, whistling snatches from the "Ride of the Valkyries," winking at Fulla as he passed her. She hesitated briefly.

Loki's voice reached out, all sweetness and honey now. "Good Fulla, as you can see, I may be busy in conference. Why don't you show our hero here to the workshop of the dwarfs, since it's there he'll work? And you might tell them they're to do whatever he says."

Fulla's protest was stopped by a nod from Odin. She came up to Leif then, jerking her head for him to follow. They went back over the same lane through the woods. She quickened her steps, marching along, head high, not looking back at him.

Leif had his stomach full of her actions. He caught up with her and spun her around. "What's going on? Just because Loki brought me here—or because you like Lee better—you don't have to treat me like dirt!"

He tried to pull her to him, but her hand came out, smacking sharply against his face. Lee would have grinned and gone ahead, and for a second Leif considered it. But the look in her eyes was too much for him. He stepped back.

"Dirt I could endure," she told him coldly. "But a tool of the Evil Companion—a trickster, a false hero—even one who looks like Balder and with whom…"

He grinned wryly. "Go on and say it. You haven't forgotten being kissed, any more than I have."

"No. I remember that—and I'll learn to hate you for it. Don't feel that you've won everything yet, Leif Svensen. Heimdallr saw through your trick."

She was pointing to his hand, and he looked down now, conscious that he was still carrying the automatic Loki had given him. Then he swore. There was no gun, but only a short stick of wood, shaped something like an automatic—another proof of Loki's power of sleight. Loki had tricked them, somehow. Yet Heimdallr hadn't been fooled, but only silenced by some persuasion of Vali. Something came into his mind—Loki's doubts about Vali and Vidarr, who would survive Ragnarok and hence might like the whole idea and the added power it would give them. He swore again and threw the stick aside.

Damn Loki! Leif scowled, wondering just what he'd gotten into. Originally, Loki was supposed to be on the side of the giants against the gods. He seemed committed to Asgard now, but maybe he was only pretending to go along here. If that were so, Leif Svensen was nicely stuck in the middle, while the millstones were grinding out trouble. To make things worse, he was apparently enough of fortune's fool to find that the only girl who'd ever appealed to him was a goddess who was determined to hate anything that Loki touched.

"All right," he told her bitterly. "So run back and tell Odin the whole story. Maybe he'll reward you for it."

"His mind is made up now. And you'll earn your own reward for your treachery when your time runs out," she said acidly.

They came out of the forest by another trail, into rough ground near the great wall, almost at the entrance of a sooty, huge building that ran back into a hill and disappeared. Fulla pointed to it. "The dwarfs are in there. Modsognir!"

A short ugly creature came out, his face covered with warts, and his whole body filthy, even to the rags that covered him. He was perhaps four feet high, but most of that was torso, and his chest expansion must have been better than sixty inches. He nodded ponderously.

"Modsognir here. Chief of armorers."

"This," Fulla told him, "is the new master of all of yon. The Alfadur commands that you obey him."

She turned quickly to leave, jerking her head up disdainfully as she swept by Leif. The little grin on her face implied that she knew she had him going and enjoyed that part of it.

It was too much. He caught her by the shoulders this time, and forced her around, pulling her to him before she could draw back her arms to slap him. She was kicking and scratching as he came, but he was pleasantly stronger than she was. Fulla tried to bury her face in his shoulder, but one of his hands in her hair forced her head around. Her lips were thin and hard. Then slowly they relaxed and parted. He pulled her closer still, letting his hand fall from her hair. She bit him.

His hands dropped completely in surprise, and she was gone, almost stumbling in a mixture of fury and embarrassment. The snickering laughter of the dwarf behind her didn't seem to help. Leif wiped the blood off his lip, but he wasn't sorry. At least she'd remember him, even with Lee around.

"You're growing," Loki's voice said behind him. He turned to see the god lounging beside the dwarf. "Fulla needs a bit of taming—as who wouldn't after being a maiden for fifty thousand years or more?"

Leif winced. He hadn't considered the fact that she was an immortal, like most of the others here. She had looked like a young girl, and he'd taken her at face value. She must have looked the same when his own ancestors were still barely able to chip flint. Maybe, though, age that produced no effect couldn't be counted. It mattered less than he would have expected. Right now, other things were filling his mind.

"I'm growing sick of it all," he told Loki. "Why should I try to do anything for this cockeyed heaven of yours? Hell, I don't even know what's true and what's fakery."

Loki smiled with his lips, but there was no amusement now in the rest of his face. "Maybe we have been a little hard on you. I suppose you're not conditioned to all this, as the men of old were. But I had to be hard on you, since I couldn't reason with the Aesir. You can't walk out on us now, though. Niflheim's no fake, I assure you."

"What is this Niflheim, anyhow?" Leif wanted to know. He had a vague idea of a cold hell, and no more. Idly, he noticed that Loki's speech sounded less stodgy now, particularly since leaving the meeting. Or maybe his ears were just getting used to the language, and he was hearing it as he would English. Probably Odin was conservative and insisted on formal rather than normal speech in council.

Loki reached into a small bag at his side and pulled out a little mirror set in a frame with a handle. "I borrowed this from Odin's possessions—without his knowledge, of course. It's a small version of the big one on his throne. Elf work—magic or science lost to us now, but very effective. A—um—I imagine that you'd call it a window through the dimensions. Look—here's Niflheim."

Leif took the mirror, looking into it curiously. Then he tried to drop it, but his hands refused to move. Something strained at his eyes, and the sight began clearing—showing people—people with—with...

The next second, he was vomiting while Loki supported him. The god had pulled the mirror out of his hand, but nothing could ease the sickness that ran through Leif. Finally he stopped the gagging and sat down shakily.

"That's the mildest part of Niflheim," Loki said, but his own voice held tinges of what Leif had felt. "It's a place where everything is wrong—and where men can't even go crazy, since it has two times, and one is fixed, immovable. The longer you look, the more you see—and that's true even though you stay there a million years. Some of the ones—but keep the mirror. You may need it to spy out how weapons are made on your world, since you and I know you're no master of the skills we need."

"Why didn't you bring in somebody who was an expert weapons maker, then? Why pick on me?"

Loki sighed. "I argued for a few trained men, but Odin and Thor would have heroes or nothing. I had difficulty persuading Thor to take one whose brother was perhaps useful to me, and more trouble arranging for the proper wounding of both together. I did the best I could, and that was hard enough."

"The best!" Leif grunted sickly. "You fixed it so I couldn't return home if you'd let me. There must be at least sixteen major crimes charged to me by now, not to mention what will happen to the farm."

"Umm. Thor protects Lee, and I'll try to do as much for you. Perhaps when the time is right I can effect some changes here and on Midgard. Let's look at your workshop."

Leif went into the building behind Loki, his legs still trembling from the shock of the quick glance of Niflheim. Whatever happened, he knew he wasn't going *there* by choice!

Then he looked around slowly from the crude forge that was being worked by hand to the hunk of iron that served as an anvil, while one of the dwarfs held the metal in his hands and another swung at it with a crude hammer. A horde of the creatures were busy working, but most of them seemed to have only their bare hands and their mouths as tools. Beside him, one was holding a crude spear head in his hands and biting off flakes of the metal to smooth it into shape.

Leif dropped back onto a soot-covered rock, staring about. This workshop made things just lovely. If he couldn't make weapons here, it would probably mean Niflheim for him and maybe for his brother. And Fulla's hate would be enough to make her look through one of the mirrors and laugh at him—at least, until Ragnarok killed off all the Aesir.

"And if I can help win your Ragnarok?" he asked.

Loki shrugged. "Then maybe you can wangle godhood and win the wench, since she's on your mind. And your world won't be destroyed then, though the Aesir will naturally take it over and run it the way they think it should be run.

Leif had a vision of what that would mean. Lord knew, men had made enough of a mess of things, but with the Aesir turned loose there, hell would really pop. It was a lovely choice—one in which even winning was an automatic losing proposition.

He came to his feet suddenly, but Loki had already stepped out of the doorway, leaving him with his problem.

CHAPTER VII

After three weeks, Leif Svensen had been able to get used to most things in Asgard. Even the daily slaughter of the einherjar no longer bothered him, since the dismembered parts always flowed together and became whole at the first touch of the nightly dew. But having to take part in the endless fracas was another matter, when he needed all his time in an effort to get some kind of weapons. To the traditions here, however, he was a hero—and heroes were supposed to spend most of their time brawling. Whenever Odin was due to inspect the combating heroes, Leif had to be present.

Now he'd found a section of the field where the dullest einherjar had drifted, and was pushing a big shield against the swords of two of them, waiting for Odin to finish inspecting a mock battle between the troops of Thor and those of Lee. There was little danger here, but it was hot work, and he was sweating uncomfortably inside his armor. A battle axe took more work than a woodsman's, he'd found, and the shield seemed to weigh a ton.

Finally, Odin left. Leif sighed and swung the big axe. One hero's head rolled across the field, to be followed by a second in another moment. Leif slung the shield across his back and hurried off the field toward a grove of trees, carefully avoiding any more heroes. It was time he got back to the shop.

But as he reached the grove, his steps slowed unconsciously. This was the place where the holy apple tree stood, and part of Fulla's duty was caring for it. He'd seen the girl there several times, though it had done him no good. Still, his eyes moved about expectantly. This time, however, there was no sign of her. The tree stood in the center of the grove, with no one about.

Leif stopped to study it for the tenth time, and the farmer in him felt sick at the sight. It was a fairly old-looking tree, but neglect more than age was responsible for its condition. Dead wood had choked off the new branches and was sapping its strength. The leaves looked sickly and yellow, and the few specimens of undeveloped fruit were small and stunted. The dirt under it smelled sour and leached out. If Asgard depended on that tree much longer, no Ragnarok was needed—the gods would never be in any condition to fight.

He sighed and finally left it, heading back to the shops of the dwarfs. There, at least, some changes had been made. The armorers had been moved out to a separate building, and the addition of a real forge, a flat anvil, some basic tools, and a crude grindstone had freed most of them for other work. The arms and armor had improved in quality for the change.

Inside the caverns the rear was filled with equipment of the same kind, but the front sections had new developments. Big metal cauldrons and hoppers were joined by queerly twisting pipes and chutes. Beside one of these, the new foreman of the dwarfs was watching two others busily shoveling crude ore into a hopper. As far as Leif could tell, there were simply two pipes leading from it, with nothing further to do the work. Yet iron sulfide went in, ran through the pipes, and came out as sulfur on one side and iron on the other.

Sudri clucked sharply and reached forward to taste the sulfur. He ground a lump between his teeth, swallowed—and scowled. He twisted the loop of pipe half a degree, dropped something into the hopper, and tasted again. This time, he burped happily. "Pure now."

Sudri had been picked by Leif as foreman for his obvious superiority to most in intelligence, and was still surprised by the honor. He looked like a maimed frog with severe glandular trouble. His nose was buried in the growths on his face, and the face was little more than a huge mouth, carried on a squat body that hopped about with grotesque joints stuck together haphazardly. The elevation above his fellows seemed to have made a new dwarf of him, however. He was almost clean.

Well, they'd have gunpowder, at least. Leif had used the dimensional mirror to find and copy an up-to-date periodic table from an abandoned college room, after his first surprise at learning that the dwarfs had a very clear idea of elements and atomic arrangements. They seemed to be natural-born chemists. They made many of their tests by tasting, but this system worked. Now he could obtain any element or simple compound he wanted from them by telling Sudri what it was.

Then he turned back toward his private room, lined with lead on the assumption that what would stop X rays might stop Heimdallr's vision. He picked up the dimensional mirror, glumly. Using it was simple enough—he only had to stare at it, thinking of any place on Earth, and the proper place would appear. Unhappily, the mirror had its limits. He could locate a library, even see the backs of the books; but until someone opened the book at the right place, he couldn't read it.

Sudri came in, expectantly. "What next, boss Leif?"

"About half a ton of U-235," Leif told him sarcastically. "Either that or some detonators."

"What are detonators?"

Leif explained as best he could, though mechanics were harder than chemistry to describe to them. They'd been mixing small batches of the gunpowder, and they had casings for grenades, since those were crude enough for the dwarfs to produce. Conceivably, grenades might even be simple enough for the einherjar to use. But getting some way to set off the grenades that would be foolproof and simple was another matter. He'd figured out ways, but none that the dwarfs could follow in their production.

Sudri scowled thoughtfully, and Leif shrugged. "Okay, I didn't really expect you to get them. Go ahead with whatever you were doing. I've got research to do."

Sudri's face cleared and he was gone. Leif picked up the mirror and began ransacking his mind for some place where a book on early weapons might be in use. West Point had been shut down because of the weather and the need of all available troops. He'd tried the stacks of the Library of Congress, but no one was using that section. Damn the limitations of the mirror! He had a book in his own library, if he could only see into the pages.

For a while, he scanned Earth at random. Things were worse since he'd last seen it. The pages of the few papers showed that military law had been imposed, and squads were trying to collect and dole out all food equally. But in the cities, thousands were already dying of hunger, or being killed for what they had hoarded. There was probably enough for all for at least a year, but it was unevenly distributed, and only time would help that, if anything would. The subzero weather and winds made it harder. Part of the newly impressed army had mutinied, to make matters worse. And squads of desperate, murderous men were spreading out from the cities into the country, looting and pillaging. There were even bands of wolves from the North that had been driven down by the weather.

Leif Svensen's own section had been lucky. They were too far from any large city, and the local administrator of military law was too busy with plans for a power coup to bother impressing food from the farmers. But even there, the less provident and the weaker were dying and being killed.

Reluctantly, Leif turned to his own farm, dreading the desolation he might see. There was a gale blowing, driving the snow across ten-foot high drifts with a force to discourage all travel. He could see nothing until he focused inside the house.

Surprise ran through him then. Everything was neatly in order, and the cellars and pantries were hardly touched. Even the livestock seemed to be doing well enough. A submachine gun and a heavy rifle were mounted beside the windows in the cupola of the house, indicating some past danger, but everything seemed quiet now. A man was asleep in the main bedroom, but he lay face down, and Leif could not see who it was. He started to swear at the figure, then reconsidered. Better a squatter who would care for things than the ruin he had expected.

Then he swore hotly as he turned to the little library. Seated in Leif's favorite chair was Loki, with a book propped on his lap. The god looked utterly content with whatever he was reading, drawing occasionally on a cigarette. A woman's arm reached over from behind him to empty the ashtray.

Leif jerked the mirror, and the scene disappeared. He started to focus on it again, and then deliberately scanned a thousand miles away. Maybe Loki had stuck him up here and was making a nice place to retreat for himself, away from the perils of Ragnarok. But there wasn't anything Leif could do about it now, and it didn't solve his problems.

Nothing else solved them, either. Study and science—other than a frantic attention to meteorology—were almost abandoned. Three weeks had passed in Asgard, but the papers confirmed that more had gone by on Earth. From what Leif had seen, and the hints he had gotten from Loki, there was no one-to-one time relationship. Sometimes things moved faster here, sometimes faster on Earth. It swung in odd jumps; but now the Earth-time was moving faster, so that a day here might be twenty-four hours there or even a month.

He found a museum with old weapons and pictures in the cases, now completely abandoned—and apparently looted for guns—but nothing that he could use. And beyond that, there was no hint to be found.

Sudri thumped on the door and stuck his head in timidly. "Almost time to eat, boss Leif. Supper due. You want me to bring milk?"

"Huh?" Leif looked at his watch, surprised to find that he had been stewing over the mirror for almost seven hours. He got up, stretching his aching muscles, and nodded. "Thanks, Sudri. Yeah, I'd better eat."

His eyes ached from his work and his back had kinks in it, but hunger was growing stronger than his other sensations. Food wasn't the best here by any means, but he looked forward to the milk.

He had found that the legendary Heidrun—the goat that gave mead— was just a plain herd of goats, giving honest milk before the gods let it ferment and mixed it with honey for the sickeningly cloying drink they used. It was like a lot of the legends—a simple thing turned into something magical in the stories. The boar that was supposed to be killed and eaten every night, to be restored by Odin's magic, had proved to be a large number of half-wild pigs running in the woods beyond Yggdrasil and killed in periodic hunts by the gods.

Boiled or roasted pork three times a day, with mead to wash it down! No wonder Odin had ulcers. Leif hadn't found any vegetables yet—though there must be some around—but he had been able to obtain a few goats for the dwarfs to milk. The stream in the back of the dwarf cave made a good place to cool and store it.

There was a halloo from outside, and Lee came clanking in. He put a platter and bucket on the bench and tossed the big shield onto the floor. "Met Reginleif coming here with the chow. She's still kicking at having to cook for you but not living with you. Oof, I'm tired. Tossing an axe around all day is hard labor."

"You might try sleeping nights, then," Leif suggested. It was a cinch that Lee wouldn't have been here this long without female companionship, and most of the goddesses and Valkyries were worth more by the pound than by the looks. But if Lee were seeing Fulla, he wasn't talking about it.

He grinned contentedly, then sobered. "I'm seeing nightmares when I sleep. Son, if we're going to have a chance of winning this war, it looks as if it's up to you. Those dopey einherjar couldn't cook sugar without someone melting it for them first. How's it going?"

Lee told him, in detail, throwing over something that looked roughly like a gun. "The barrel inside that looks as if a dyspeptic caterpillar had crawled through butter. It took a dozen dwarfs four days, even so. I'm still trying to get a lathe built, but just try cutting threads on anything with no guide and no decent tools to start with."

"So the grenades look like the best bet, eh?" Lee threw the useless gun aside. "Even if you get them made, though, I'm not too sure how well they'll work against the giants, from what Thor and Tyr tell me. Thor's son Ullr—no, wait a minute, he's Thor's stepson—anyhow, he's a pretty nice guy and a damned fine bowman—he wants to meet you, by the way..."

Leif grinned in spite of himself. "Here, stop eyeing the milk and help yourself. Maybe you'll remember what you were saying then?"

"Thanks." Lee swallowed gratefully, draining the mug and refilling it. "Ullr says Odin's getting impatient. He didn't like your not coming to mess with the other heroes, and now you've been holing up here three weeks with no results."

They were interrupted by Sudri, who was followed by a bent, grizzled old dwarf, whose grey skin indicated that he was one of the stone dwarfs. "Andvari," Sudri announced importantly. "Andvari, make some detonators for the boss Leif."

Andvari tucked a chunk of flint into his mouth, followed it with a reddish dust, chewed busily, and swallowed. A moment later, he coughed it up and spat two or three hundred tiny crystals into his open hand. Sudri picked one from the bunch, put it into a powder-filled grenade casing, and squeezed the hole in the iron closed with his fist.

Lee gulped, but Leif was used to such things. Someday he'd have to find what these original inhabitants of Asgard were made of; it obviously wasn't protoplasm. But now he gestured for the grenade. "How's it work?"

"You throw it. After it gets thrown, it explodes when it hits something. But not when you don't want. Works a little by thinking—the way white elf tricks once did."

Lee took the grenade and moved to the entrance. He heaved the object strongly, and it banged against a rock, with no results. Sudri recovered it at once.

"I didn't want it to go off that time," Lee explained. "But this time, if Sudri's right, it should go boom." He threw it again, ducking as the explosion split the air and threw pieces of rock over the landscape. Obviously, it worked! "Leif, I think you've got the weapon. Better make up a batch and send them over to Thor's place for me to demonstrate. It should keep the gods happy for a while. I'll go spread the word."

He picked up his shield and headed toward the palace Thor called Bilskirnir, while Andvari and Sudri started back into the cave for supplies. Then Sudri stopped to point to a heavy leather bag. "Chemicals and stuff you wanted are ready, boss Leif."

CHAPTER VIII

Leif stared at the bag doubtfully. Then he shrugged and went inside to don his armor again. When he came out, the dwarfs were busy making grenades under the direction of Sudri, while Andvari sat spitting out detonators. Leif tucked the automatic Lee had returned to him into his pocket and went to the doorway. The tiny sun was sinking, from the diffused glow of the clouds to the west, and the air was cool and pleasant after the closeness of the caves. The dew had fallen some time before.

Off to the side, barely within vision, he could make out the lesser Valkyries and the more energetic einherjar pairing off. Beyond that lay Thor's Bilskirnir, the most pretentious building next to that of Odin's. Leif grunted as he saw someone walking toward it, a figure that might be Fulla.

There was a sudden barking from the direction of the forest, and he saw Rex galloping toward him, just as the dog seemed to catch sight of him. The next second, he was being pounced on, while a wet tongue ran over his face. Leif staggered backward, grabbing for the dog. Then he stopped.

"All right, Loki, come off it."

The dog disappeared, leaving Loki in its place, looking surprised and carrying a bundle in one arm. The god shook his head. "Either you're getting used to illusions, Leif, or I'm losing such skill at sleight as I have."

Rex would have made a whining sound in his throat, but Leif kept the information to himself, letting Loki puzzle over his detection. "What's happened to Rex, anyhow?"

"He's been in a fight with Odin's pet wolves, and Thor's hard at work patching him up." Loki chuckled. "Thor's more interested in the dog than in the grenades Lee says you have made."

Leif started to tell how the grenades were made, only to stop as Loki drew out a pack of cigarettes and began tearing off the paper. He put a white cylinder to his lips and shoved the pack back in his pouch to draw out matches. Leif caught his hand.

"Not in here, or you'll blow the place up. Pick up any habits you like, Loki, but don't fool with gunpowder."

He'd spoken more sharply than he meant, partly because his mouth had begun watering at the sight of the smokes. Loki made no comment until they were away from the cave. Then the god grinned faintly.

"It seems gunpowder would explode no sooner than you do, Leif," he said "Here, take this bundle. I brought you and Lee each six cartons. Since you're in no mood to be—to be needled, as you say, take them now."

Leif could feel his face redden, even as the welcome taste of the smoke cooled some of his resentment. He'd probably still been nursing some of his doubts about what he'd seen of his home through the mirror. On a sudden decision, he reported it to Loki.

The god nodded. "Look longer next time. I told you I'd try to protect your property, and I usually keep my word—in spite of what has been said about me. I've convinced your neighbors that the wolf was a real one, not Rex, and that Lee was the one mixed up in the fighting rather than you. For a few pigs you could spare, they're ready to forget a lot there now. And Faulkner, who was starving at his own place, has taken over the care of yours."

"He seems to be doing a good job," Lee admitted. But he found himself surprisingly less interested in the farm now than in the difficulties here. It would do little good to worry about one farm when the whole world was somehow to be destroyed if the gods lost Ragnarok. Even a world ruled by the Aesir might be better than no world. "Loki, why can t you bring some of the tools I need, the same as the cigarettes? If a Valkyr could carry me, why not a hundred pounds of equipment?"

"Metal. It resists the twists of Bifrost. Your automatic and watch were harder to bring than you—and should have been removed, if Reginleif had thought. Hoof-Tosser can carry two men, but it took two other Valkyries and their horses to get you and your metal here. Even half a pound is a heavy load."

"They carry armor," Leif pointed out.

"That's elf stuff, not true metal. When Odin led the Aesir through Bifrost long ago, it was easier. Then Asgard seemed downhill from your earth, but now it is reversed.

There were nine worlds connected through Bifrost then. Now only Jotunheim, Muspellheim and Niflheim are easy to reach. Your world is closing to us, except for eddies such as now make travel possible. Vanaheim and Alfheim—the home of the white elves—are completely closed."

Leif let it go. He was learning that Loki's logic was above traditions, and if he said it couldn't be done, there was no use trying the idea on others here. He puzzled again over the contrast between what mythology he remembered and the facts. There seemed to be logical solutions just out of reach behind all the magic. It was like the shoes of the Valkyries' horses. The elves had made them, and somehow they could harden the air into a firm roadway back from Asgard, but nobody knew how; even the few surviving elves in Asgard no longer understood it.

There was another error in the mythology that bothered him. "How come Fulla takes care of the tree? I thought it was…"

"Idunn's task," Loki finished. "It was, when she remembered. There was a time with a giant named Thjazi when the apples were lost by her—though she blamed that on me. This last time it was a fanatic priest of some new religion you still have. The Valkyries picked him up as a hero. Dying, he refused the elf flesh and had to be brought raging through Bifrost in his own flesh. Then he quieted down and turned poet as well as hero. Bragi—he's the verse-cryer—took him in, and Idunn was all too willing to be kind to her husband's guest. The priest left her sleeping, took the best of apples, and was halfway into Niflheim's depths before we suspected."

Leif stared at Loki, unbelievingly. It was an impossible thing. He hadn't even been able to look at the place.

"I said he was a fanatic," Loki said. "Tyr tried to follow, and he's no weakling, but it was too much for him. So—well, we slept through a thousand years for want of the apples until the tree bloomed again and wakened us with its scent. But before we slept, Odin widened the gateway and Thor tossed Idunn into Niflheim after her priest. Now Fulla has the job."

And not much luck with it, Leif thought. He wondered whether the all-important apples were necessary, like vitamins, or only a habit-forming drug. But at least normal life seemed impossible here without them. "Why didn't you grow more than one tree?"

Loki grimaced. "We tried, but the seed never grew a tree with the proper fruit. From your books, I find that is only natural, but we knew nothing of grafting. And it's too late for that here and now. Some say the giants are already approaching. There's been an eagle flying around—a huge one. Some of my changes of form are illusion, but the giant folk actually can change their shape with some effort. So this may be a spy, though it was too far away for even Heimdallr to see its true nature."

"I've got a gift for Heimdallr," Leif said, suddenly remembering. He pulled a little telescope from his pocket. Even though Sudri had shaped it according to Leif's sketches in his bare hands over a small fire, it showed a surprisingly clear image. "Maybe if you tell him it will improve his sight, he'll gloat about that instead of trying to spy on me all the time."

Loki examined it thoughtfully, trying it out. "A good trick. Give him more to brag about and he'll be your friend for life—as much as he can be. All right, I'm off with it. And good luck with the tree."

The god made a quick motion and again the form of Rex appeared, running off swiftly into the night.

Leif picked up the leather bag Sudri had prepared and struck out through the dim light, heading for the place where the sacred apple tree was. Loki had guessed right, though he hoped none of the others got the idea—they were suspicious enough of new ideas to kill first and examine afterwards.

It was as nearly completely dark as Asgard ever became when he reached the place. Against the glow of the sky, he could see the worn old limbs and the weeds around it. He cleared the land with one of the new tools and began spading in lime and fertilizer which the dwarfs had made to his specifications. The feel of the earth was a welcome relief, after the crazy labors he'd been mixed up in.

He finished with that finally, and began carrying water in the leather sack, washing the fertilizer in. Sometimes now he even began to believe that the gods must win this crazy war. Afterwards—well, he had his one wish. Maybe something could be done with it. And he was no longer sure that the gods could really take over the earth, even if they tried. They were a lot less powerful than he'd thought at first. Certainly they were lousy horticulturists!

He climbed into the tree and began sawing off the dead wood, pruning it back. It was a small tree, completely unimpressive, and the work was less troublesome than he'd expected. He found one branch where part had already been cut. Had Loki already tried to prime it? If so, he'd mistakenly taken a living branch instead of a dead one, but it would do no harm. Leif moved about, protected from scratches by his armor, painting tar over the cuts. Finally he hauled the brushwood away and stood back, examining the tree again from the ground. It looked lean and plucked now, but the dead wood wouldn't sap all its energy, and the ground would nourish it.

He rolled the spade and saw into the sack and headed down the trail. Luck had been with him. None of the gods had spotted him, and Heimdallr was probably busy with other things, not looking this close to the center of Asgard.

He turned around a bend in the path and collided sharply with the figure of a woman! Then, as he bent to help her up, he saw that it was Fulla.

CHAPTER IX

Fulla was moaning slightly as Leif Svensen lifted her, and she winced as he started to release her. Then she stood upright and he took his hands away. Maybe, if he turned quickly, she wouldn't recognize him. She might suspect, but she couldn't prove anything.

She started to step toward him, and moaned again, stumbling. He paused, irresolute, but only for a moment. The next second he had scooped her up into his arms and was carrying her off the trail, to a spot where he'd seen a smooth, mossy section a few days before. As he moved with her, she glanced up, and he realized that his face must show against the sky. Perhaps it wouldn't be enough for recognition, but...

She jerked a little, before settling back against his armor.

"What's wrong?" he asked, as he dropped her gently onto the moss.

"It's my ankle. I twisted it. It's nothing—it'll be all right in a few minutes." She winced again as his fumbling fingers undid her sandal and began rubbing the ankle. He moved his hand away, but her hand moved it back. "No, don't stop. It hurt at first, but now it feels comforting, Lee."

Lee! Of course—Lee and Leif looked and sounded alike, except that their attitudes colored their expressions. He was puzzled over her guess, though, until the clinking of his armor penetrated his senses. It explained things well enough—he hadn't been wearing it except when he had to, after the first day, while Lee had apparently grown into his. She must have guessed by that. At least, he could hope it was more than just an expression of her wishes.

"Better?" he asked.

"Mmm. Sit here, Lee. I thought you were with Gefjun tonight. She'll be jealous if she knows you're out alone—or worse, if she finds you with me."

Leif grinned, remembering Gefjun, another of the maiden goddesses. So Lee had been doing all right, even if he hadn't been meeting Fulla. He tried to call up some of Lee's mannerisms. "Let her be jealous, Fulla. Who kissed me first—you or Gefjun? Or is that something you've forgotten?"

"No." She slid downward and closer to him. After the unwashed naturalness of most of the females in Asgard, he was surprised to notice that her hair was faintly and pleasantly fragrant. "I began to wonder if you hadn't forgotten that kiss, though."

"I've got a long memory for pleasant things, Fulla." It was no good, being mistaken for another man, but it was better than not being noticed at all. The armor was suddenly hot around him, and he was sweating. He reached for the buckles.

She bent to help him with it, and her hands were caressing. At last the heavy mail was off, and she was closer. Her voice was a whisper now. "I haven't forgotten anything, Lee. But even a goddess can't remember one kiss forever."

He tried to laugh as Lee would have laughed. It sounded hollow to him, and the blood was pounding in his ears until the sound must blur even the laugh, but she didn't seem to notice anything wrong. "There should be a moon now," he tried to say lightly as he bent forward. "With that, maybe this Asgard of yours could be a true paradise."

"I could beg Odin for a moon for you," she murmured. "Or two or more. But can't the moon you want wait?"

The moon had nothing to do with anything, though, as he discovered. This was already a paradise—a strange, bitter paradise. He tried to forget that she thought he was Lee—to pretend she was saying these things to Leif—and he failed; but even that bitterness couldn't steal all the pleasure from him.

She sighed softly as he withdrew his lips reluctantly, letting them break slowly from hers. Then her arms tightened again, and she was pulling him down, her mouth demanding. She strained tautly against him as his hand tightened on her back, and her body turned slowly, bringing the flat of her hips against him.

"Oh, Leif! Leif!"

For a second there was only the caress of her voice, small and hoarse in the darkness. Then the words penetrated. He jerked abruptly away, freeing her. "You know me?"

She shuddered, pulling herself slowly up and doing something to her hair. Leif fumbled for a cigarette, and he could see her face white and tense in the light of the match. Her eyes widened as he drew in the smoke, but it was unimportant to her now. Her lashes were dropping as the match went out, her fingers twisting into odd shapes. Her voice was tiny and lost in the space around them.

"I knew, Leif. After a twining—and I went too far with the spell on me to escape—after a twining, there can never be any mistake about the other. You knew me, and you couldn't have seen me in the darkness."

It was true enough, he realized. He had sensed who she was, rather than seen. For whatever it was, this twining seemed to have worked on him. She waited, as if asking for help before she went on, but there was nothing he could say. And finally she went on slowly.

"I saw you going this way—and I started to follow, to watch you—to try and hate you. Then I couldn't just see you and not speak—so I went back. But I came, after all. I thought I'd never find you! And I didn't hurt my ankle—or even stumble into you by accident."

"But why the act about Lee, then?"

"I had a plan—I thought. If I met you and you thought I took you for Lee…Then it really wouldn't count." Her voice was even lower now, and he bent to listen. "I know how you felt, or I thought I did. And I wanted you to suffer. I couldn't mix with Loki's treason, but if you thought it was Lee I—I liked…somehow, it would be all right for me, then. And you'd be even more miserable afterwards. Oh, Leif, I…"

She dropped her head against his shoulder weakly. "And then—then I couldn't pretend. You should hate me, Leif."

He tossed the cigarette aside and turned to her. "I could. I don't."

She sighed, slowly, relaxing back onto the moss. "Fifty thousand years is a long time to wait." She pushed the hair back from his head, her long fingers lingering and trembling faintly. "But I'm glad I waited. I'm glad you forced the twining, my beloved."

He would have told her his own feelings, but dawn was creeping up. "We'd better be getting back," he told her. "I should have taken you home hours ago."

She nodded, but pulled his arms around her again, snuggling against his shoulder. Her cheek rubbed against his arm, and he lifted one hand to the back of her neck, drawing his fingers around and past the lobe of her ears. Suddenly he felt her body stiffen. She began drawing back, her hand slowly going to her breast, as she slid out of his arms.

"My tree!"

He'd forgotten the blasted tree, but he looked now. Seen in the full light of day, it was a bleak sight, with most of its branches missing, and the thinness of its foliage showing fully. Every scar he'd put on it stood out clearly. Its poor development and age showed now where the false density of branches had hidden the worst before. And more than ever, the meagerness of its poor crop showed to the world.

Then another gasp came from Fulla, and he looked down to see her staring at the sack sprawled on the trail with the saw he had used showing plainly.

There was disbelief in her voice. "You! You ruined the tree—the life of Asgard! My charge…and I—I…"

He caught her shoulders, pulling her around to face him. "Of course I did, Fulla. It was dying from the deadwood and from lack of food in the soil. I did it for the sake of Asgard, to give us more chance for strength at

Ragnarok. No—I did it because I couldn't see you failing your job when I could help. Damn it, I did it because I was in love with you!"

"My tree!" She sagged in his hands, slipping out of them and falling to her knees on the moss. Her eyes remained fixed on the tree, and there were tears in them, while sobs slowly began to wrack her body. "And I trusted you—I loved you. Oh, don't worry, Loki's companion. You succeeded in your plan. After this night, I can't report you to the fury of the Aesir. You made sure of that! But I hate you, hate you, hate…"

"Fulla!" He bent toward her, but she screamed.

"Don't you dare touch me!"

"Fulla, you said you loved me. Can you love me and jump to the first wrong conclusion against me—on circumstantial evidence? Will you listen, let me show you what I did and why I did it? Or are you going to go on believing every lie your fears can cook up? Come here, and I'll prove…"

He bent again, and this time she didn't scream. Instead, she turned viciously, swinging her right hand—which now had a rock in it.

Leif stood back coldly, spitting out a tooth and blood, without feeling the blow. He was numb and empty.

"All right, Fulla. Tell your damned gods, if you like. Tell them the part you want, and I won't blackmail you with the rest. Send me to Niflheim, if that will fill your mind with anything more than spite. And when you find what a fool you've been, remember I tried to tell you the truth—and that I did love you. I thought you were someone a man could count on. I had no real reason, but I thought a lot of damned fool things. I should have known you were only a goddess, like Frigg, and no good without your pedestal. Go climb back on it, then. And if you ever want me, whistle, but don't hold your breath till I come running! I'm through being pushed around by a girl who couldn't get herself a husband for fifty thousand years!"

He picked up the sack and slapped it over his shoulder without looking at her. Her painful sobbing went on as he turned down the trail, and something in him hated the sound and ached to go back and still it. The larger part of him was frozen with hurt and anger, and a wish to return ache for pain. Love without respect and trust might do for the gods, but Leif Svensen wanted more than that out of life.

Heimdallr and Loki were doing the impossible by standing together without quarreling at the foot of the path as he came out of the woods, but he barely noticed that the self-styled son of nine mothers was busily polishing the little telescope and smiling at him. He nodded toward them curtly and went grimly on, heading for the workshop. Sudri would look good to him after what he had been through.

"Leif." Loki was running to catch up with him. "Arrooo! I'd better get our Lady Fir to bandage that lip. It looks as if Thor had hit you."

"Grin just once more, Loki," Leif told him, "and you'll wish Thor had been the one to hit *you*."

Loki blinked and stepped back, his eyes shrewdly appraising. A touch of malicious amusement showed on his lips. "Oho! So. And our farmer is suddenly turned into a berserk hero. Well, Odin will be happy…"

His grin slipped off as Leif moved toward him. There was a haze in the air and a rattlesnake drew back ugly fangs and made threatening lunges where Loki had been. Leif did not hesitate. He pulled out the automatic, willing himself to see the true form of Loki, and a dim image seemed to form around the snake. He raised the automatic and aimed for the head.

The snake snapped out of existence to reveal Loki again, this time without a trace of amusement. "Enough, Leif. Sometimes I talk like a fool. Let me take that back."

The anger suddenly evaporated from Leif, taking most of the numbness with it. Only the pain was left. He could feel the starch running out of his system, and made no effort to stiffen again. Loki's eyes were sympathetic now, as he clapped Leif gently on the back.

"There was a girl once—about so high…he said quietly, indicating the point of his chin, but there was a curious edge to his voice. "Only she didn't stay that high. Giants mature at the same height as men and gods, but like the snakes of old, they keep growing. Sigyn was twenty-one feet tall when we last tried to live together. She called me a ridiculous runt and threw me out. Yet it is strange how I still think of the girl she was—and how she took care of me when I was under the venom punishment, yet could no longer look at me or speak to me. There was a twining there too, perhaps. Well…"

Something like the boom of thunder crossed with the crack of a board breaking rolled over them then, in sound waves that were physical enough to pluck the leaves off the trees. Leif snapped out of his trance.

His worst fears proved true. Above the dwarf cave entrance, a plume of smoke was rising, with a billowing cloud under it that still contained rubble and falling stones. The powder there had obviously exploded, all at once.

CHAPTER X

A picture of Sudri's mis-assorted body coming down in sections jumped into Leif's mind, and his legs began moving. Loki looked startled, and then came along, matching his leaps. They swept over a rise of ground, and were among the hillocks—darting among boulders and onto the path, while the acridly sweet smell of powder hit their noses.

Leif gave a sick look to the leaning timbers, and then was inside. A yelling voice reached him, and he turned toward it. Sudri was bent over the broken form of Andvari, shouting in the glottal stops and Bantu-like clicks of the stone dwarf dialect, which even the power of Asgard could not make understandable to anyone but a dwarf. The mouth of the old dwarf just barely moved in reply.

Surprisingly, the damage hadn't been so great as Leif had feared. The solid stone wall separating the front section from the rear still stood, and the explosion had reached only the front entrance and wooden outer building. There were no other bodies.

Sudri saw him then and faced him. "Someone came in and threw a grenade. I yelled. Andvari held back the detonator. It was still partly his to control. We all went to the back, but he had to stay. He was too old to hold it long, or carry it far enough, and it went off. More powder went off. But most powder was already in grenades, stored in the rear. You see how it is."

Leif nodded and turned to the old dwarf, whose pain-filled eyes were raised to his. "Who?"

Sudri shrugged, but the old one motioned, and Leif bent over. There was a gasp as the stone dwarf fought with the unfamiliar soft sounds so foreign to his speech. But he formed them, his eyes showing surprise at the question, and Leif heard.

"Vali Odinsson!"

"I'll remember that, Andvari," Leif promised. The old eyes remained fixed on him, and the hand came up in a gesture that might have been meant for a blessing. Then the dwarf dropped back, dead before his head touched the floor.

Sudri touched Leif reassuringly. "Don't worry about the detonators, boss Leif. Andvari told me the trick in his speech. I don't understand it all, but any stone dwarf will know. We have lots of detonators already."

The foreman turned, shouting back, while the cowering dwarfs began to come out, staring at the wreckage. "You Bifur, Nori, Modsognir, Onarr, Mjodvitnir, Vindalfr, Fundinn, Throin—you fix things. We'll be back in production in about three hours, boss Leif."

"Yeah," Leif said, still staring at the old dwarf. He'd only seen the grim old figure a few minutes, yet the death hurt. Leif wondered what he himself would have done had he been left with a bomb he could delay but not stop. And afterward, would his only thought have been to pass on necessary knowledge? There was more to the creatures than the ugly body of one could indicate.

Damn Vali!

He heard the sound of others behind him, and swiveled on his heel to face the crowd that was collecting. "Lee, you can stay if you like—Thor too. The rest of you get the hell out of here before I set Sudri's crew on you with grenades. Gods, heroes, whatever you are, get out of here! And from now on, anyone who comes too near these caves—even Odin himself—without my okay gets a grenade in his guts."

Thor came up, stern questions in his eyes. "Those are dangerous words, Leif Svensen. Why?"

Loki spoke quickly into the ear of the black-bearded god, and Thor nodded. "So? Then they are good words. I have little use for a leader who will not fight for his men, even if they're only dwarfs. Back, all of you— back before I try my hammer on you!"

Leif could see Fulla mixed into the crowd that was watching, her eyes darting toward the entrance and striking his. He tightened his lips and swung back to the cleanup job that was going on. A moment later, he saw her moving off, up the path toward her tree, while the crowd grudgingly moved back to a satisfactory distance.

Vali! It would do no good to confront him, since he was one of Odin's sons, and Leif had nothing but the word of a dying old dwarf, heard by himself and apparently by Loki. Or had it been only Vali? He'd warned Loki about the danger from a spark here, and Loki had been familiar with what a grenade could do. Leif no longer wanted to distrust the god, but he couldn't completely forget the legends and the opinions of many here.

"Look!" Loki took his arm, turning him about and pointing. High above, gliding like a vulture, a dim speck showed in the sky. From it came a harsh, mocking cry. "The eagle—and much too big for the height at which he is soaring. It must be a spying giant."

"Fine," Leif commented. "At least he knows we have boom stuff now. He didn't set it off, though. All right, Sudri, carry Andvari's body back gently. We'll bury him in whatever rite his people use. Lee, sometimes I'd like to be one of those blooming berserkers. But there's nothing you can do here, if you've got other business."

"I'm supposed to demonstrate the grenades to the gods," Lee said. For once, his face was serious, and he tipped his helmet as he passed the body of Andvari. "Let me know if you need help. And if they want, I'd like to attend their rites for him."

Leif moved back through the caverns, examining the packed grenades that hadn't gone off. Production had been fine. This was a perfect example of the type of weapon the dwarfs could make, needing only a rough shell, without fine machining. He kicked at a small sack on the floor and swore at its weight. He stooped to examine it just as Sudri came rushing up.

"No!" The dwarf darted under him, waving excited hands. "Bad stuff, boss Leif. It's okay for dwarfs, but not for humans. That's the U-235 you ordered. Half a ton. It keeps better in small pieces like this."

Leif gulped thickly and drew back. "It does, Sudri—it certainly does."

He should have known better than to try sarcasm on a dwarf; he'd mentioned the stuff, it was an existent isotope—so here it was. Half a ton of it, probably of perfect purity, in little bags of less than critical mass. How did the dwarfs know that? And knowing it, what did the gods need of humans to show them how to beat the Ragnarok? Then he realized that the gods would never think of seeking advice from a dwarf. And even knowledge wasn't necessary here. In gathering it, some dwarf probably had put too much together in one sack. It couldn't be made to explode by being brought beyond critical mass slowly—but it would begin radiating. Probably the dwarfs would never think of driving two subcritical masses together instantly, before their own heat could boil them away. Only men would have use for such facts. Yet he wasn't sure. The dwarfs were apparently radiation-immune, but they had been able to see that it was dangerous for men.

He watched them storing it away carefully, then went back to superintend the reconstruction. Idly, he heard the detonation of grenades, and wondered how the gods were impressed by Lee's display. There were explosions again, followed by a long, sustained yell.

The walls were almost whole once more when Reginleif came toward the caves, stopping well beyond the entrance and announcing herself by a loud halloo.

"Odin demands you at once, Leif Svensen!" she yelled. Her face was sterm with disapproval.

Leif shrugged and moved out, with Loki behind him. Now what? They'd probably heard about the tree—unless it was something even worse.

"If I don't come back, Sudri," he called, "look me up in Niflheim."

But it wasn't a very humorous crack. It had too much probable truth in it.

CHAPTER XI

There was a dense crowd collected at the judging place before Yg-gdrasil, and Leif Svensen scanned their expressions, trying to estimate the seriousness of the charges. It didn't look good. Loki whistled faintly in surprise as he stared at the Aesir, confirming Leif's fears.

Frigg was speaking to Odin, and her righteousness was all too evident, even from a distance. Beside their father, Vali and Vidarr were nodding vigorously at what she said. Odin's shoulders were slumped more than usual, but they straightened as he saw Leif coming, and a gesture cut off the words around him. Heimdallr was intently polishing the lens of his new telescope, and his face was totally inscrutable.

Fulla sat at the foot of Frigg's dais, her face lowered. She glanced up at the stir around her, and her eyes met Leif's for a moment. Something that might have been the beginning of a wan smile touched her lips, but it vanished as he stared back at her coldly.

Lee Svensen moved promptly to be beside his brother, and Thor lifted his body and followed, holding Rex in one hand, the big hammer in the other. A lithe young husky whom Leif recognized as Thor's stepson, Ullr, scratched his head and moved doubtfully after them. They lined up beside Leif and Loki.

"Tell them all to go to hell," Lee whispered.

It was more likely to be the other way, Leif decided. The very fact that he was getting such obvious support was welcome—particularly from Thor—but it indicated that the ones rallying to him were sure he was in desperate need of help!

Odin's voice cut off any chance to ask for information.

"Leif, Son of Sven, a time has come for judging. There is treason in Asgard. I have promised my son Thor that your words shall be heard and justice rendered. But how shall we believe one who is sponsored by Loki as a hero, yet who spends little time on the field where the heroes practice their skills? Nevertheless, speak and defend yourself before we pass our judgment against you."

Thor let out a bellow of indignation, probably provoked by Lee's quick commentary on the unfairness of the words. But Leif cut in before the god could speak. The sickness of Fulla's lack of trust, and of Vali's murder of

Andvari was back inside him, and he was tired of bowing to the will of such gods as these.

"With such justice as you offer, Odin, what's the use of saying anything? When the judge is biased, there is no justice. Well, I'm not surprised. I've had one sample of the justice of Asgard already this morning. I should have expected something like this. But at least tell me what in hell I'm supposed to have done. If you mean the explosion in the workshop, there *was* treason enough—against me and my workers! On that, you might try cleaning the filth from your own household before you clean outside it."

He saw Fulla's eyes wince at the reference to the morning, but he snapped his gaze back quickly to Odin, whose one eye seemed to be shining from a thundercloud. It was no way to address the ruler of the gods, and Odin seemed unable to accept the words as having been spoken. Vali came to his feet, his ferret-face tautening. Leif stared at him, then spat on the ground, and rubbed the spot out with his foot. But the son of Odin only grinned nastily.

"You are accused of trying to destroy the einherjar," his bland voice announced. "At the accusation of Vidarr and myself. The grenades which you furnished your twin behaved well enough, to be sure. The others were also claimed to be safe when not thrown with the intent to destroy. By good fortune, before it was too late, Vidarr and I decided that a more suitable test was needful. We demanded the right to test other grenades. Behold the result when we threw them at a group of the heroes!"

Leif's eyes followed the pointing finger to a rough cloth upon which a gory mess had been gathered.

Odin took up the tale as Vali dropped back into his seat. "Fifty or more loyal einherjar, Leif, Son of Sven! From but two of those creations of yours, thrown by my sons. Nor can all my skill hope to restore them to life again, scattered as they are. Shall we gather at Vigridr for the Ragnarok to find that our weapons shall remove our heroes, leaving us defenseless before the Sons of the Wolf? Shall we let you continue to make devices which are meant to kill at the touch of a hero? Nor docs it seem that your treason stops there, from what my ears have but now told me. But speak. We are patient, until judgment is made!"

It was obvious that Vali and Vidarr had willed the grenades to explode, but Odin would never believe in such treachery so close to the throne. Leif turned his eyes to Loki, but the god was staring intently back down the trail toward the shops. Niflheim pressed close, and Leif could feel the sickness that vision had given him before in looking at the distorted world. He turned to Lee, to see his brother holding a single grenade in one hand, doubtfully fingering it as he tried to estimate the chances. It wouldn't work, Leif knew.

Thor was on their side now, but he would certainly permit no such action. Leif was surprised that Thor had not already switched back to Odin.

Still, he eyed the grenade. If he could get it and move back where it wouldn't hurt his small group of friends, it could at least destroy him so completely that they could never send him to Niflheim. Compared to that place, death would be most pleasant.

He moved slowly toward Lee, facing Odin again. "Why should I scream protests that you've already told me you wouldn't believe? What good would it do? All right, so the grenades wiped out some of your heroes because they were used falsely by your sons. And so I did mess around with the sacred tree of yours, though…"

Fulla was suddenly erect, screaming something at him, but the clamor of the others drowned out her words. Leif slipped the few remaining feet to his brother and reached toward the grenade. Now if he had time to get into clear space…

"More grenades, boss Leif?" Sudri's voice asked roughly beside him.

He twisted his head to see the dwarfs lined up beside the little group around him. Loki was grinning, rubbing his hand over a grenade, and the dwarfs all held weapons of their own. But before Leif could adjust his mind to the new factor, Loki's voice cut through the din.

"It would seem that the question is now whether this Leif Svensen *can* be sent to Niflheim safely, Odin," he shouted. "There are those present who feel that justice has not yet been rendered, and among them is Oku-Thor himself. You have seen what two of these grenades can do. We have scores of them, and the skill to use them, which it would seem Vali and Vidarr lacked. Am I right, Thor?"

Thor was troubled, but nonetheless determined. He nodded. "The grenades worked properly when I tried them, as well as Mjollnir itself. Until the facts are entirely clear, and decisions fairly rendered, this man has my protection, Father Odin. I demand true justice."

Surprisingly, Heimdallr was coming toward them, pulling a huge sword from its scabbard. There was nothing foppish about him now; the softness seemed to have vanished, and the sword was a living thing in his hand. He took his place as far from Loki as he could, but clearly was lining himself up behind Leif.

Fulla had also left the front and was moving to them, but she hesitated, and then sank down again.

"But the tree!" Odin was unused to having his court divided, and uncertain of the menace confronting him. Tradition made no provision for this, and his anger had given place to hurt. Most of the other gods were shifting unhappily about, not knowing what to do. "Thor, you heard him admit to defiling the tree."

"Then I say send someone to the tree to examine the damage first, and judge later!"

Heimdallr waved his big sword casually. "No need. I've been watching the tree through this bit of magic which your warlock rightly thought useful to only one of my skill." He pulled the telescope out and stared through it, preening himself a bit as the attention of all focused on him. Leif couldn't see how his sight could penetrate through the obstacles between him and the tree, or how the telescope could help there; perhaps it was extrasensory sight, and the telescope only helped psychologically. But Heimdallr seemed satisfied.

"New shoots come forth and the apples are ripe," he announced. "It would seem that Leif Svensen has certain skills with such affairs."

Another yell went up from the gods, and the ravens suddenly shot from Odin's shoulders, darting out toward the tree. Fulla's face abruptly came to beaming life, and she sprang toward Leif.

He grinned crookedly, thinking that he might have expected this. Now that the weather was clearing, she wanted to be out in the sun. He turned his back on her, facing the forthright figure of Thor.

He wasn't too surprised when the ravens came back, each with a yellow apple in its beak. They seemed full-sized now, and looked like winter greenings, firm and ready for eating. Time here could do strange things, it seemed, such as compressing the normal processes of months into a few hours. By rights, the fruit should have ripened by now—and hence, once given a chance, it was fully ripened now.

Odin took one of the apples, smelled it, and bit into it. He bit again, and ten years seemed to fall from his shoulders. Others were heading toward the apple, but he motioned them back.

"Leif Svensen, you have permission to come forward and stand beside us."

Vali screamed angrily, but Odin motioned him hotly to silence. Leif was unsure, but Loki's hand thrust him forward, and he moved up to the seat, mounting the little dais. Odin's hand reached out with the apple, and there was a clear invitation on the god's face.

Reaction was hitting at Leif, making his legs tremble as he stood there, and the bravado that had somehow lasted through all the danger was gone. But as he managed to control his teeth and bite down on the apple, a sudden raw current of power rushed through him. He swallowed automatically while a warmth and strength diffused over him. He'd doubted the real help of the apples, but he could no longer question it. Whatever they contained, it was powerful stuff, with the feeling of vitality to it.

"For this, Leif Svensen," Odin told him, "I would gladly forfeit many respects and forgive many acts. The returning to us of the power of the tree was no act of treason, nor could a traitor have done it. And because of that, I am moved to accept Loki's explanation that it was but lack of skill in the hands of my sons which caused the grenade to wreak such evil. Or perhaps the influence of the spying eagle Heimdallr has seen."

He paused, studying the council, keeping them waiting for their turn at the apples while he considered. At last he sighed. "The matter of some of the Aesir turning away from me is a very grave offense, but there was some justice on their side. We are all overwrought, and even I may have been hasty—as you were in the anger at our distrust. Go back to your work, Leif Svensen, and we shall consider the events of this day to have struck a balance."

Leif stepped down, considering. But this was no time to press the treason of Vali. He slipped back, letting his eyes flick across Fulla's face quickly, and rejoined Loki. The god was turning the dwarfs back hastily toward the shop, and Leif realized it might go ill with them if they stayed around to remind the Aesir that they had come out to rescue him. He began leading them off, while the gods clustered around Odin, waiting their turn for the apples. Odin was belatedly being overly fair, making sure that those who had supported Leif Svensen received the same preference as the others.

CHAPTER XII

Loki joined Leif before he reached the workshop, and Ullr was with him.

"The youngster has brought forth something which is unexpected among the Aesir," the god announced, grinning. "He has created an idea! And by now, Leif, you know how rare that is, and why I spend so much time with you. Well, out with it, Ullr."

The young god fondled his bow and furrowed his forehead. "I was thinking that those grenades are good things— but even better would be arrows, made hollow, and with the same stuff inside, to explode as they hit. Could that be done?"

Leif took the arrow he held out and examined it, surprised that Ullr had developed a second idea—that of making models before he submitted his first idea. This arrow was thicker than most he'd seen, apparently made of some reed and covered with thin gold to give it weight. "Did you test this to see how well this shot?"

"It worked, but I had no explosive."

The scheme seemed possible. The dwarfs could produce crude sheet metal, and they could even weld it in some mysterious way. The inside of the arrow wouldn't have to be perfect for this purpose, provided it was ground straight, and in balance on the outside. Leif passed it to Sudri, who nodded his big head while his mouth opened in a grin that went three-quarters of the way around his neck. He called up other dwarfs and set them to making such arrows.

Later, Leif watched Ullr go off with Loki to try out the new arrows. Since they wouldn't explode until wanted, the same ones could be used again and again for target practice. He turned back to his private office, rebuilt and relined by now. On impulse, he stripped his wristwatch off and handed it to Sudri.

"Thanks for coming to help me, Sudri."

The dwarf gobbled incoherently, strapping the watch onto his thick wrist and listening to it tick. He'd been fascinated by it since he'd first learned its purpose. Leif grinned and shut the door after him.

He picked up the mirror and stared into it, jerking it quickly past his eyes. But even the brief glimpse of Niflheim was too much. Shuddering, he put the mirror away. Well, he'd passed the first crisis, and he knew who his friends were.

Loki apparently could be trusted in a pinch; the trouble was that he was the most intelligent of the gods and the only one with any sense of humor. He preferred wit to muscles, and his choice must often have led him into the tricks of which the legends accused him; but it also put him firmly on the side of anyone who could meet with him on the same grounds. Thor was a god of absolutes. He could be trusted completely so long as someone didn't pull the wool over his eyes. Ullr was so hopped up about his new invention that he'd go to any lengths, practically, for the man who could get the arrows made for him. And Heimdallr was more or less on Leif's side—though his foreknowledge of the condition of the tree made his position less certain.

But the rest of the Aesir would probably be just that much more against Leif Svensen because of the split that had occurred. They wouldn't like the idea of having a mere man challenge them and get away with it. Odin might be happy now with his apples, but the best that could be said for the day was that it had produced another truce. And there was the combination of Vali, Vidarr and Frigg lined up squarely against him. The more he succeeded, the more they would oppose him.

The next time, there wouldn't be any convenient coincidence of the apples to sway the Aesir's decision.

He got up as a halloo sounded from outside and went out for his supper. Then he stopped in the doorway, staring. Reginleif had been replaced by Fulla. Well, why not? Wasn't he the boy who had saved her precious tree and hence assured her of a job?

He cursed the weakness in him that made his hands tremble as he took the bucket and platter from her.

"The apples are gathered and in my chest," she told him, touching a small basket at her side—too small to contain more than a few apples, it seemed. "And I have been studying a new art. Lee has told me that you wanted vegetables, and I have found them. They are here in this—this stew. I— I've never eaten stew."

He stared into the bucket, noticing that there was something that looked like cabbage and carrots mixed with the rest, as well as grain to thicken it. By rights, he should have refused her bribe for his favor again, but his mouth watered at the sight, and he needed his food as much as any hero. "Wait a minute," he told her.

He went inside, to come back a minute later. "I've taken half of it— that's plenty. You might as well have what's left. It's better than straight meat for your complexion, anyhow."

She'd seized the bucket as if to dump out its contents, but now she stared at him, dumbfounded. One hand rose to her face, as if she were testing her skin. Then she let it fall to her side. Without a word, she turned and moved off toward the main buildings.

Drat women, goddesses or otherwise! Leif clumped back in and started to eat the stew. With some of the salt the dwarfs had made, it wasn't too bad, but each mouthful was harder to swallow than the one before. Finally he pushed it aside and picked up the mirror.

He found what he was searching for at last, and carefully watched operations that were supposed to be so secret that not a hundred men knew them fully. Weapons were still being made against the possibility of aggression or revolt, it seemed. And obviously the making of fission bombs had been simplified considerably since he'd read the college descriptions of them. In a pinch, the dwarfs could turn them out. The means for bringing the two masses of U-235 together violently weren't too difficult, and the same trick detonator would set off the charge that started the whole operation.

Just what could be done with them when they were made was another matter, though it seemed a shame to have all that power lying around without using it. He grimaced at his own ideas, wondering how many other men had felt the same about their weapons, and how many wars and deaths it had caused. But in this case, of course, it was justified.

He tasted the stew again, muttered to himself, and began putting on his armor. The trouble was, he needed some company. Reginleif had indicated she would be happy to share his time, but he had no desire to see any woman now. Loki he saw enough, and there was never any sure way of finding him. And that left him only Lee and the whole company of almost-human heroes, minor gods, and others who were filled with nothing but brawling, and were the natural group to come under Thor's protection.

He clumped out, starting automatically along the trail that led to the tree, and then swore again as he struck out firmly for Bilskirnir.

Reginleif brought his next few meals to him, but the vegetables and better cooking continued. He was sure the Valkyr wasn't responsible, but if Fulla was preparing the food, she gave promise of being a fair natural cook. The food improved steadily and began to develop a certain amount of variety. Leif Svensen heard that stories were circulating about the unheroic fare he ate, and he avoided Loki's eyes when the god was around at the arrival of meals—which was often, since Loki was beginning to pick up tastes far removed from Asgard.

But the work in the shops was doing well enough. The grenades were stacked up now beyond any reason to make more, and a good supply of the explosive arrows had been made. Leif cudgeled his head for ideas and went on trying to find hints in what little the mirror could spy out for him.

But he knew that he was only wasting time now, while he delayed the final decision on the U-235. Finally, he had to decide, and he called the dwarfs in and outlined what was needed. The bombs were within the range of their powers, though he had no way to test the first ones to be finished. He was doubtful of how much use they would be, for that matter. Still, it kept the shop busy, and satisfied the gods that he was making progress. It might even prove helpful, in case of further trouble, to have a surprise to spring on Asgard.

The group at Thor's proved to be as dull as his own company, since Lee Svensen was chiefly worried about some means of getting a measure of efficiency out of the heroes, and Thor's lack of humor grew ponderous in time. Leif tried spying out the news back on earth by reading whatever papers were being published, but he found himself more and more uninterested. The weather had apparently reached its worst and settled down to stay. Meteorologists had given up trying to explain it. Wherever the conditions permitted, there was a wave of cultism growing, but the cold prevented the wide spread of that, just as it ruined the hopes of most of the local dictators. The cities were horrors now, and some parts of the country were little better. A heavy fall of snow was reported in equatorial Africa, but generally the air seemed to have purged itself of most of its moisture, and little fell elsewhere.

There was nothing there to cheer him, except for Loki's word that it was traditionally supposed to be even worse. In the primitive societies that wrote down the original accounts, that might have been better fulfilled, but modern man was too used to depending on a steady stream of trade to revert easily to the practices of the raider of old.

Finally, when Reginleif brought a rather good meat loaf with vegetables on the side, Leif gave up. He told himself he was heartily sick of being reminded of the fool he'd been, and that something was going to have to be done about it. He'd see Fulla once and for all, and take care of things properly. Anyhow, the way to his heart wasn't really through his stomach. He'd see her, though.

He felt better as he buckled on his armor and went out the doorway.

Then he paused. Coming toward him in the gathering twilight, with a happy little smile on her lips, was Fulla. Beside her, Vali strode along, motioning down toward the shop. They were still a couple of hundred yards away, but obviously heading toward him. Leif started to duck back, just as Vali caught her arm. Leif was puzzling over the meaning of the two together when a sudden cry from above jerked his head up.

Huge against the remaining light of the sky, the giant eagle was plummeting down, headed straight for the two. Leif fumbled for his automatic, yelling, but Fulla had seen it already, and was trying to run. The wings of the bird suddenly shot out, stopping its fall, and it dove toward her, blotting her from Leif's sight. Then it was lifting. Fulla was clutched firmly in its talons, and the chest that somehow held all the apples was still buckled to her waist.

Leif fired at it, knowing the distance was too great, and took a shot at the running figure of Vali—futilely. He could see the eagle rising rapidly now, heading out toward the great wall. Another cry came from its beak, and it began to struggle heavily. There was a coruscating flash of rainbow fire, and the eagle and Fulla seemed to dwindle into nothing.

It had crossed Bifrost into Jotunheim, taking Fulla *and* the apples with it!

CHAPTER XIII

For a frozen second, Leif Svensen stood there, cursing himself. It was obvious that Vali had told Fulla some trumped-up tale about Leif's wanting to see her, and she had been coming to a tryst that would have been pointless if he'd stopped being a pig-headed fool sooner and gone to her when he first wanted to. Now, without the apples, the gods would be sleeping pushovers for the giants, leaving Bifrost wide open for them to get on to Earth. He'd seen enough of the giants through the mirror to know what that would mean.

He'd never been sure he could help to win Ragnarok, but he'd done a nice job of insuring its being lost—in the worst possible way.

Then he swiveled and dashed back to the shop, tossing savage commands to Sudri and grabbing for the mirror. He took one quick look, spotted Fulla and the eagle in Jotunheim, and tucked the glass into his pocket. Sudri was pelting away toward Bilskirnir as Leif came out and struck across the field at a full run, cursing the weight of his armor but having no time to remove it.

He could smell the stables as he came near them, and he turned in hastily. Reginleif was busy currying one of the horses, while the goddess Gna was watching. Leif grabbed Gna's shoulder and swung her around. "Which is Hoof-Tosser?"

She started to protest, but her eyes had tipped him off. He dropped her and headed for the horse—a magnificent white stallion, bigger than any Percheron that Leif had ever seen, but built with the fineness of line of an Arabian. Gna came after him, trying to hold him back, but he had no time for fooling. He planted his fist under her chin, watched her crumple, and faced Reginleif. The Valkyr blinked, squirmed as the automatic came out and centered on her, and then pulled herself together and went in for the horse.

"Saddle him!"

She obeyed, and Leif drew near the horse. Hoof-Tosser was skittish, but Leif knew horses. He gentled the animal, forcing the tension out of his voice and speaking softly into the stallion's ears. Then he swung into the saddle, lifted Hoof-Tosser onto his rear legs, and pivoted about and out of the stable.

He headed straight for the wall, wondering how to steer a horse up-wards. He wasn't even certain that the animal could lift into the air, except on Earth, as it was mythically supposed to. But it seemed to understand when he drew back on both reins, and made a convulsive leap. A second later it was airborne. Leif Svensen had no idea of how to cross Bifrost or whether the armor he wore would cause trouble, but it was too late to worry now.

"Jotunheim, Hoof-Tosser," he ordered.

The horse whickered, then drew back its head and screamed. Leif tried to imitate the sound, and realized it wasn't unlike the cry Reginleif had giv-en in going from Earth. Probably sonics had some effect on the dimensional bridge. Already the air was taking on the rainbow ripples he remembered. His armor was growing warm, and the automatic was almost hot. There was a queer twisting resistance, but the steps of the horse didn't falter this time. Loki had been right in saying that entrance was easier to the other worlds than it was to Earth.

Under him, Asgard turned to nothing but color ripples that disappeared in turn; Leif looked down to see a cold gray landscape under him, scraggy with huge boulders, and looking like something left over from a period of glaciation. He glanced at the mirror now, twisting it until he could find the giant. But it refused to work—naturally, since it worked only between the dimensions!

Far ahead, there was a victorious scream, such as a bird might make, and Leif headed the horse toward it. But though Hoof-Tosser went on eat-ing up the distance, he could see nothing of his object. He shook his head, to swing suddenly at a call beside him.

For a second, he thought it was the eagle, only to realize that this was a great hawk. Hoof-Tosser whickered, and the hawk drew up. "You're head-ed right, Leif," Loki's voice called.

The hawk somehow landed on the horse's back, and began to struggle. A fine membrane seemed to peel off, and Loki emerged from it, stuffing a small bundle into a pouch he wore. "Freyja's hawk garment—elf work at its best. Do you know what you're getting into?"

Leif shook his head.

"I can't help you," Loki told him. "At least, not inside one of their forts. They'd smell Asgard on me. You may be able to pass. Look, Sudri only barely told me that you were off after Fulla and the apples. Who's responsible?"

Leif told him, and the god cursed in violent stone dwarf speech. He began to fill Leif in as best he could on the general habits of the frost gi-ants, wasting no time on anything but the most practical details. Most of the knowledge was not encouraging. Then he pointed down, and Leif could see a rugged castle below, apparently hewn out of one of the great boulders. He made out a lighted courtyard of some kind.

Loki had the reins of Hoof-Tosser and was urging him down. "We'd best land yonder, and you walk the rest of the way. I'll try to conceal Hoof-Tosser and work my way close. If you get free with the maid, whistle three times and the horse will come. Don't worry about me—if I am left, I can find my way back. Just get Fulla and her basket to Asgard—those apples are our first worry! Even over her, Leif!"

Leif slipped from the horse's back, shaking his head as Loki held out a sword to him. He'd had some sword practice since coming to Asgard, but he'd do far better with just the automatic. And if he was lucky, maybe he wouldn't even need that. These were the giants stationed near Bifrost, picked to resemble the Aesir to aid in spying on them—and through their own careful breeding, he would not be too much unlike some of them. According to Loki, the barely mature giants were no bigger than a man. He might be able to pass as a young giant.

Getting into the castle proved easy enough. There was a spillway for rain water or something like it on one side, and he hoisted himself up and through the wall. Light shone out from an opened door, and there was no one in the courtyard. From inside, however, there was an excited babble of giant voices. Leif gritted his teeth and stepped in as if he had business in the home of the giants. No one was looking at him.

All he could see was a plain of twisted, hairy legs blocking the door, and supporting a massive body. Then they moved, and through them Leif could see bits of giants and chairs, and something at the far end that looked like a glass case with a big sword in it. The top of it was suddenly opened by a huge hand, and Fulla's chest of apples dropped beside the sword. There was a hoarse bellow of laughter, and Fulla's voice shrieked.

Leif twisted through the legs of the giant and moved into the room, an immense place, well packed with giants of all sizes and types, some with tusks, others with long fangs, and a few that looked almost human in a bestial way. None were deformed in the sense that the dwarfs were, but all had a basic coarseness about them. The hair was too thick, even for their bodies, their worst features always too prominent, and their expressions a blend of imbecility and sadism. Leif knew that some were smart enough, but none looked it.

All were intently watching a thirty-foot giant at the head of the table, who was casually holding Fulla in one hand. The other hand came out, swishing the thick hairs on the knuckles across her face. She flinched, twisted her head, and spotted Leif.

She covered the expression almost at once, but it had betrayed her, and was like a finger pointing at Leif. The giant over him looked down and yelped. "Balder!" Leif Svensen felt a taloned hand suddenly grab at his middle, and he was sailing fifty feet through the air. "Hey, Skirnir!"

The giant who'd held Fulla reached out a hand and caught Leif. The breath whistled from his body, and his ribs creaked, but the hand had cushioned the shock. The giant turned him over, staring out of narrowed eyes. "Hmm. No, not Balder, though he looks something like the pretty one. He must be a new one. He doesn't smell like a hero, either—real flesh. Thought I'd learned every As when I was a kid spying on them as Freyr's messenger." He bent closer, letting his foul breath blow across Leif. "Did Balder have any sons?"

There was a roar at that. "Balder!" one of the giants repeated. "Sons." And they were off again.

From the back, a croaking bellow came, and Leif saw something that was neither eagle nor giant, but turning slowly from one to the other. The thing croaked again, and its head became all giant. "It's the warlock—Leif they call him. Hai—Vali said he'd follow after the girl."

"Of course I came," Leif yelled. The quiver that was running through him wouldn't show so much if he bellowed back at them. "As a warlock—Witolf's kin—do you think I'd work willingly for the Aesir? When all the confusion came up, I lit out over Bifrost for your group on the double."

Skirnir laughed heartily, slapping his thigh. He wasn't bad-looking, as giants went, in spite of his size, and he was unlike all the others in wearing a smile. But under it, there was something that Leif Svensen had seen only in the eyes of a man who had tried to beat a dog to death. That man had been smiling, too, until Leif had lost his temper for the first time in his life and somehow knocked him unconscious.

"It won't work, warlock. We heard of you from Vali and Vidarr. Here, since you love the wench, join her. We won't separate you. We'll roast you together, and after you tell us of Asgard, I personally will eat both of you. How's that for real uniting?"

He chuckled at his humor. Fulla moved toward Leif, her legs tottering under her. Leif's were in little better condition. He was reasonably sure the giants didn't eat people— at least, not the frost giants—but a lot surer of the sadism behind the taunt. Fulla's eyes were hell-wracked as she slumped against a big mug beside him.

"I got you into this. Oh, Leif, I'm such a..."

Then she screamed, and Leif saw Skirnir picking up a huge ember in a pair of tongs. He began moving it toward them. Leif reached for his automatic, yanked it frantically out and squeezed the trigger. Nothing happened! He'd forgotten to reload. Skirnir had started to duck, dropping the ember which fell on another giant and brought forth monstrous yells. Now the head giant grinned again. He flicked the gun from Leif's hands and pulled the pouch of clips away in a snapping motion.

He stuffed both the automatic and ammunition into the case with the sword and apples and then pulled the gun out again to examine it. It was too small for him, but he seemed satisfied. With a malicious grin, he threw it back to Leif and reached for another ember.

A bellow came from the rear, cutting off the enjoyment Skirnir was getting from everything. One of the smaller giants rushed up, tossing Loki's helmet onto the table. "Aesir!"

Skirnir frowned. "Damn! Vidarr swore he'd send them to Muspelheim after Surtr's tribe. No matter, they can't be in full strength, or they'd have struck. Here, Hrymr, throw these two into the cage and get our horses. We'll have to look into this."

Hrymr grabbed Leif and Fulla in hands that resembled steam shovels and began dragging them off. All three of his mouths were drooling as he tightened his grip. But a bellow from Skirnir ended whatever ideas he had. He clumped behind the case, into a series of corridors, down some stone steps, and back to a cave covered by a huge oak door. There he tossed Leif in quickly and sent Fulla after him. She landed with a thud that threatened Leif's already-aching ribs.

The big door swung shut firmly with a positive click of the lock, leaving the cell completely dark, while the giant's footsteps sounded off toward the others.

Leif groaned, and Fulla began to roll off him, taking more time than seemed necessary in the process. She left one arm over his chest, and her lips were beside his ear. "Leif, I'm scared."

He chuckled dryly, forcing himself up on one elbow. "Then that makes two of us. I'm afraid I wasn't cut out for this sort of thing."

He got to his feet and lifted her to hers, testing himself and finding no broken bones. He was surprised to notice that the weakness wasn't bothering his legs now; apparently he was getting used to being afraid. But he still couldn't laugh at danger, as Lee did. Then suddenly he realized he had laughed—and wondered whether the heroes might not be laughing at their own knowledge of fear.

Beside him, Fulla caught her breath, snuggling against him. The warmly personal scent of her hair penetrated, even over the musty odor of the cell. He pulled her closer, his lips tautening in a twisted smile. If the giants were coming back soon, he'd probably be screaming in agony too intense for thoughts of her within the hour, but he didn't have to die now in anticipation. The future couldn't take away the pleasure of the present, at least, and only a fool would do less living than he could while life still stirred in him. He caught her chin, and found her lips in the darkness.

For a minute, it seemed to work; then a vision of Skirnir smiling and moving the ember forward captured his mind. He drew back, grimacing. This was a hell of a time to be billing and cooing—particularly when he had no way of knowing what sort of jam Loki might be in.

"We've got to get out of here," he told her. "As soon as I can get a light to see what the setup is…"

But Fulla sighed softly, reaching out a hand from which all the trembling had vanished. She took the matches he'd been striking futilely and thrust them back into one of his pockets. "There's no air for the flame sticks to burn on Jotunheim, Leif. We only seem to hear with our ears and to breathe because Bifrost adjusted us to Jotunheim in passing over. And the fire the giants have is magic. But I don't mind the darkness or what the giants will do, as long as you're not angry with me any more. You do like me now, don't you?"

"I do, kid," he told her. In spite of the fifty-thousand years she had lived, she was still only the twenty-year-old girl she seemed, at heart.

He felt his matches again, wondering. The idea that there was no air didn't impress him. If there had been none, there would have been no need for all the things that made it seem there was—and the matches should still have sparkled briefly in the dark. It was probably just a tale the giants had told once to keep others out of Jotunheim. No air, no breath, no live. Then, when someone had tried it and found that it wasn't fatal—probably Loki—the giants had been forced to invent a whole passel of lies to cover up. And since both the giants and Aesir were ready to believe in wonders, they had all probably wound up believing in the alleged absence of air.

For a moment, he wondered about the whole Ragnarok business. Could it all have been a giant trick—a prophecy designed to create what it prophesied? It seemed possible, though it would no longer matter. Both sides were so tradition-bound that they would still go through the motions even if all reason were removed.

Fulla stirred against him, making a purring sound in her throat. "Even if you had ruined the tree and killed the Aesir, I'd still be yours. It wasn't my heart that hated you, and hit you, Leif—it was all the old traditions that die so hard. But after you went away with a frozen face, I knew that tradition didn't matter. Only then you were so cold and distant…Leif, why did you come to rescue me? I'd caused you so much trouble already!"

"Shh." He'd never had much use for story heroes who dropped their important business to go rescuing some clinging vine from the villain, but it seemed natural enough now. It was probably a tradition as deep in his race as the traditions of the gods and giants—traditions that could hold back Ragnarok for the right signs, even when the giants could have found Asgard asleep and undefended. Or maybe it was because he was responsible, and he'd had to develop a sense of stubborn responsibility in the long years of running the farm by himself.

"Shh," he repeated. "I'm not sorry."

It was the right answer, and she leaned against him, content. Or as nearly so as a woman can ever be. "I must look a mess, now. And just when my complexion seemed to be improving, too. If I only had a light and a mirror…"

His sudden yell cut off the words, and he was fumbling in his pocket, cursing himself. Of all the darned fools, forgetting the dimensional mirror! Somewhere in a big city on Earth, there'd be a searchlight he could locate. His mind directed the focusing, letting it draw gradually closer, while a growing beam of light began to lance from the mirror surface, strengthening as his focus came closer to the light. The massive walls of the cell sprang into view.

He swung the light over them, finding no trace of weakness anywhere. And the door was solid, locked on the other side with a bolt that couldn't be reached. His heart sank for a moment, then he grunted. It was supported on four bronze hinges, each fastened with three brass screws instead of the pegged construction he had expected. The giants had more technology than he had thought.

"Hold the light on the door," he told Fulla, giving her the mirror. He drew out the automatic, forcing himself to concentrate on the mirror focus without deliberate thought. There were things about the gun's army design that the giants hadn't suspected, such as the fact that it was specifically made to be its own toolkit. Even without shells, it was useful. He began disassembling it rapidly.

Finally the rod that served as a screwdriver lay in his hand. It was apparently pitifully weak and slim, but the metal in it was sound, and brass screws turn easier than iron ones. He found bits of rock to prop up the door and take the weight off the hinges, then began working on the first screw. It was rough going, and his hands ached with the effort of forcing the screws, but they turned. In a few minutes, the last screw dropped into his hands, and Fulla cooed admiringly, reaching for the door.

He shook his head, massaging his fingers until he could reassemble the automatic. They'd have to reach the case to get the apples; and once there, a new clip would make the gun his best chance for getting free.

The door moved reluctantly as he heaved at a cross piece, and began to swing in. He took its weight on his shoulders, somehow easing it down to the floor. Maybe there was supposed to be no air, and hence no real sound—but if he'd thought he heard Hrymr's footsteps before, then the giants might think they had heard a loud noise from a falling door.

Leif Svensen wiped the sweat from his forehead, and peered out into the corridor; it seemed free, and he reached his hand back for Fulla. They crept forward cautiously, but the place seemed deserted. He began dashing down a long passage, just as a figure stepped out of one of the side corridors.

Leif brought the automatic up without thinking, but a quick whisper reached him. "Leif! Hold it!"

"Loki!" Fulla moved forward to the god, making a few quick gestures, and nodded. "It is you, and not a deception. We thought you were caught."

"Too bad I wasn't, eh, Fulla?" Loki asked, grinning at her. Then he made a whistling gesture without sound. "Well, what's this? You seem almost glad to see me. Leif, you'll have the wench tamed yet. No, they didn't catch me—I used the helmet to distract them when they had you almost on the fire. I slipped in here under illusion to save you. I can't hold the trick long here, though, so you found me in my own form. Come on."

He'd been moving forward as he whispered to them. Leif gripped his shoulder silently, and the god grunted, accepting the gesture properly as thanks. He led them around a complicated course, quite different from the way Hrymr had come, but a few minutes later they were cautiously edging out behind the case holding the apples and ammunition.

"Luck," Loki commented. "No giants. Open it!"

Leif lifted the lid—and a sudden clangor began from a big hammer beating on a brass gong imbedded in the floor. The giants had a warning system, and already he could hear yells from outside. The big creatures would be here in seconds—long before the three could reach the door!

CHAPTER XIV

Loki had already snatched out the things from the case. He tossed the chest of apples to Fulla, handed her the sword with a look of surprise and near awe, and gave Leif the clips. Leif began shoving one in at a run toward the door, while Fulla swung the great blade experimentally. It seemed to be light and almost paper thin, but amazingly tough, passing through the leg of the case without apparent resistance.

"Freyr's sword!" She was unquestionably reverent as she held it. "The great weapon here!"

Leif Svensen could remember snatches about it. It was one of three or four of the final, perfected weapons the elves had given the gods. This was supposed to be a weapon to make Excalibur look like a kitchen knife, and it almost looked the part.

Now there was a louder clamor outside, and giants began boiling in, answering the gong. They came shoving through the door, ranging from ten to thirty feet in height, forming a solid wall of swords and spears as they charged at a full run toward the three in the middle of the room. Leif brought up the automatic, but he knew it was futile to try it against that amount of brawn.

Hrymr clapped two of his mouths together in surprise as the bullet hit his chest, but the spear in his hands rose to throwing position without a tremor and started for Leif.

Something whipped past Leif's head from behind, just as Loki's hand caught him and dragged him down beside Fulla, flat on the floor. Then the room shook to an explosion, and Loki was bouncing to his feet again. Where Hrymr had stood, there was only a gory mess, and the giants were backing away, except for a few who were making no further plans due to sudden death.

"I've still got two more grenades," Loki said grimly. "With enough luck, we may be able to get outside where it's dark enough that we can hide. After that... Come on, we've got to find cover before they strike again."

He led them at a run across the huge floor, dragging the corpses of four of the giants into a crude barricade. Fulla looked sick at the idea of dropping onto that, but she dropped with the others, when the giants started forward again. The giants were not all fools. They'd learned their lesson; this time, Skirnir was sending them in well scattered, to minimize the effect of the grenades. The main attack was by spears, and the floor behind the three trembled as the heavy weapons landed. But the corpses seemed to give enough protection—at least until some bright giant decided to try a forty-five degree angle cast.

Leif was shooting carefully, taking his time and aiming for their throats. The big torso seemed unharmed by a .45 slug, and the heads were protected by massive layers of bone. He reloaded, counting three more clips. Loki waited until several in advance came close together, and finally threw the second grenade.

Skirnir yelled, but it caught several of them. This time, though, the giants made a forward rush as soon as the explosion ended, and Loki was barely able to get the final grenade thrown in time to halt the leaders.

The giants hesitated, and Loki nodded. "Next, they'll loose the rest of the spears, and then charge. Here, this one had a sword you can manage. Keep low—in a brawl, sometimes, being shorter has advantages. Strike to cut their tendons, and then into their throats when they fall. Fulla, I'm calling Hoof-Tosser. If he can get through to us, grab him, and get to Asgard."

She gripped the amazingly versatile sword and shook her head. "I can kill giants with this."

"You scram!" Leif ordered harshly. He heard Loki let out a piercing whistle, keeping his eyes on the giants, who were already drawing back their spears.

Hoof-Tosser suddenly crashed through the door, high and coming fast, with his feet beating down at the giants' heads. For seconds, it disconcerted them, and the horse dropped. Leif made a sweep as his arm came around and threw Fulla into the saddle. The horse rose at a yell from Loki. It was becoming obvious that the animal was more than just a flying horse—he seemed to have a fair understanding of events and instructions.

Then the spears fell, one grazing against Leif and catching in the cloth of his trousers. He yanked free, as the giants came boring in, and was over the barricade with Loki.

They were lucky enough to dart into the thick of the charge before the giants realized they were coming, and Leif began struggling to stay with Loki and avoid the giant legs at the same time. The god was right—since the giants had difficulty in separating enough to get a clean sweep at the pair. Leif chopped out with the sword, ducked as a giant started to fall, and managed to drag the point across the huge flabby abdomen, disemboweling the creature as it fell. He was surprised as he saw how well Loki was doing. But even the legends had never made a coward or a poor fighter of the sly god, and there had to be some reason for Thor's willingness to put up with him, as he seemed to have done. Beside them, there was a snick of metal against bone as Loki's sword found a throat on another fallen giant.

But that gave the opening the giants needed. Leif felt a huge hand dart forward, leaped to avoid it, and found himself in another hand, with Loki also encircled. There was an end to their fighting, almost before it really began.

Then the hand suddenly opened, and the giant began falling, his head jumping from his shoulders toward the floor— and Leif's eyes darted up to see Fulla coming down again on Hoof-Tosser, the sword drawn back for another swing.

And a deafening roar from the doorway seemed to shake the whole room and drag every giant around. Fear washed over most of the big faces before they had time to look.

"Thor!" Loki yelled. "Get behind that barricade and lie close, before we get trampled. When Thor's really an-..."

Leif snatched a glimpse of Hoof-Tosser carrying Fulla toward the doorway, before he dropped beside Loki. Thor's fighting bellow came again, and there was a deep, hollow sound that could only be his hammer finding a giant skull. Almost on its heel, the sound of a grenade came, followed by another. There was a sudden thump of giant feet, and the first giant leaped over the bodies shielding Leif and Loki.

Leif's sword leaped up, and the giant landed with a stumble, to fall on his face, and start crawling away on hands and knees. The tendons on his heels were sliced through.

"Good man," Loki said approvingly, and his own sword licked out. To the giants, Thor must be sheer catastrophe; none even bothered to turn back for a swipe at the two striking them, but collapsed only to start crawling desperately for the rear.

Then the fight ended, and Thor was over the bodies, dragging Leif and Loki to their feet and shoving a bag of grenades at them. The first of the giants had just reached the exit when Leif's toss crumpled him. A minute later, there were only parts of giants lying around.

Lee came running up. "Okay? God, son, you had us worried when we couldn't see you among those giants. Say, Fulla, come on down and let's see one of those apples."

She was dropping already, and Leif accepted the fruit gladly. He could hardly stand and hold the sword now, though it had seemed a part of him during the fight. But the first bite of the apple sent its usual heady strength through him, and he managed a fair grin as he watched Fulla put what was left back. The chest was more of the elf work, apparently, since it could hold the entire crop of fruit without difficulty, prevent spoilage, and still take up little more space than his own pouch. Perhaps it really stored its contents in some tiny dimension of its own.

He was surprised to see even Thor wiping sweat from his forehead and waiting for the effects of the apple to wash over him. He looked around, nodding at Leif. "Without the grenades, things might have gone less well. They were more than tenfold in numbers than should be in a giant fort. Ho, you'll do, Leif Svensen. There's a place for you on the right side when the Sons of the Wolf come down at Ragnarok, if you want it!"

Leif realized that Thor was handing out the highest accolade he could, and apologizing for his comments that first time at the tree. Somehow, he felt like a peasant who had just been knighted by a king. This queer tradition of theirs began to get in the blood in time. But Thor cut off his thanks by lifting Fulla from Hoof-Tosser and into Leif's arms, then picking both of them up and carrying them toward a tank of liquid at the side.

"And a maid worthy of a berserker," the big god rumbled, in his closest approach to humor. "But my goats won't like the stink of giants on you!"

He doused them into the tank and out again, rumbling what was probably meant for a laugh, then seized Loki and treated him the same. They came out surprisingly clean, and almost instantly dry.

"How'd you reach us?" Leif asked.

Lee grinned. "We were already following Sudri's story when Vidarr came up with a big tale about giants from Muspelheim. Everybody else went off there, but I persuaded Thor that there was a lot better reason to trust the dwarf."

They went out into the courtyard then, where Thor's two goats were waiting, each slightly larger than a Holstein bull. Thor climbed to the front of the vehicle to which they were hitched, looked back to see all were accounted for, and yelled. They were off at full speed, with Hoof-Tosser trotting along at their side. Loki and Lee stood beside Thor, looking forward, and Leif and Fulla were alone at the rear. But he was too tired to do more than hold her close quietly, and she seemed content to fit his mood. It was over an hour later when Thor's bellow rang out, and they began crossing through Bifrost, to pelt over the sward toward the judgment tree.

Thor's yell sounded again, and the gods scattered to let him through. Leif grabbed the reins of Hoof-Tosser and vaulted into the saddle, unfinished business bringing new strength to his body. He stared through the crowd, noticing that Odin and several others were missing, but his eyes searched for Vali and Vidarr.

Then he spotted them, off at the side, between Odin's seat and a small pile of grenades that Odin was keeping for his personal testing. Their faces were incredulous, but hardening into sudden decision as they turned toward the grenades. Leif reached for the gun, to find it twisted in his pocket.

Thor shouted, and the hammer cut the air with a scream that left a wake of steam behind it, lifting Vidarr from his feet and literally splashing him against the tree. But Vali had reached the grenades and scooped one up before Leif's gun was fully out, or Thor's hammer could return.

Vali was confident now, his rat-face smirking. "Safe conduct, Thor, on your honor, or the lovely Fulla and the apples will be supping with Balder! You've won now, but…"

The gun in Leif's hand spoke sharply, and Vali's face blanched as the grenade fell from the pierced right hand. Thor's hammer came up, but Leif was remembering Andvari and his promise, as well as the danger to Fulla. "Mine, Thor!"

Thor nodded. "Yours, Leif Svensen!"

Hoof-Tosser was already in the air, overtaking the running Vali. Leif brought the horse down, kicked as carefully as he could at the treacherous god's head, and was off, gathering the thin figure up and lifting it in front of him, just ahead of the saddle. Fortunately, the blow had only stunned Vali briefly. His eyes were opening as Hoof-Tosser began lifting up and into Bifrost at Leif's shout.

Hoof-Tosser screamed, but this time it was more in protest than to break the veil through the bridge. Leif ordered again, and the horse seemed to hunch himself.

Then all hell was tearing at Leif's mind, and even the horse seemed to feel the same. Vali screamed and began to struggle, to cease in a paralysis of fright and horror in the ripples of dark color that began to die down. Leif closed his eyes, but the hell still poured over him. He held back his vocal chords, savagely fighting to keep them from ordering Hoof-Tosser back, and summoned the last desperate effort of his will. Hoof-Tosser was making a sound no horse should make, but he was still moving ahead. There was apparently little gravity here as Leif lifted Vali over his head and tossed the former god forward and into the thick of his new surroundings.

Then Leif found he could no longer speak to order Hoof-Tosser back; but the horse had had enough, and suddenly reversed of his own will.

Niflheim's cold fingers released reluctantly, but Leif's eyes were frozen shut, and his mind teetered and gibbered at him, even when the voices of the gods were around him again. He felt hands reaching for him, but he was already passing out.

Fulla was cradling him, and there was the taste of apple and something bitter and strange on his tongue when his mind began creeping back. His brain had mercifully refused to remember anything clearly; somewhere, there would always be a section of scarred memory from the few minutes, but its very horror had burned all connections to his consciousness. He grinned feebly at Fulla and looked up to see Odin on the seat, finishing some remark to Frigg. The eyes of Odin's wife were frozen lightning as they stayed fixed on Leif.

The Alfadur looked older and more beaten than usual, but he was holding the hell of the treachery of two sons to himself, and Leif was surprised to see no anger in the god's eye. Odin watched Leif rise and nodded wearily. "I have removed the bum of Niflheim, Son of Sven, in small gratitude for saving me the need of meting out such justice as one of those I called son might merit. Henceforth, by virtue of all that has happened on this day, be known as Leif Odinsson!"

There were incredulous sounds from the other gods, and Frigg screamed, her hands contracting to claws as she turned to Odin. Leif shook his head and looked to Loki for explanation.

Loki's expression was both puzzled and more sardonic than usual. "That makes you an official god, Leif, adopted by Odin himself. But don't get any ideas—Odin probably did it to spite Frigg for siding with Vidarr and Vali so long. And there are catches to it—it doesn't mean you are any freer. You're bound now to win Ragnarok more than ever, or you'll join Vali as a traitor. And it usually takes several thousand years before you begin to develop whatever powers you may grow beyond that which you already have, so you're still a god in name only!"

Put that way, it was easier to believe. Leif liked Thor's honor better than this empty one. But Odin had finally quieted Frigg and was speaking again.

"And lest Loki make you think this is a mockery, though it is the only honor we have to give, all former oaths apply. Should we win Ragnarok, the boon of which I swore is still yours to ask. With that, and your place as my son, you can gain powers beyond most others."

He shook his head slowly, stepping down from his seat and approaching Leif. The arm the god laid on Leif's shoulder was a tired one, and Leif felt a stirring of sympathy that deepened as Odin went on in a low voice. "But to the son who replaces two unnatural ones, I admit victory seems most unlikely. The giants now know of our new powers, and the Gaping Wolf already seems to course beside the dog Garm, while my eyes saw the hordes of Surtr assembling in Muspelheim. We have won back a weapon worth ten thousand einherjar, since the sword of Freyr must be with us at the final battle. But without Vidarr, who shall kill the Wolf when I have been swallowed? Thor, Leif! I grow weary. Lend me your strength as I go to Mimir's well to read what shall come of the future now."

Leif Svensen shook his head slowly, conscious of the ever-amazing surprises of this paradoxical world. He looked at the icy, venomous face of Frigg, and back to the god who'd given one eye to learn only that he must rule with the certainty of eventual defeat—and to whom being swallowed was a lesser evil among the dire things to come. Suddenly, Leif had enough of it.

"Father Odin," he asked, "as Leif Odinsson, do I have a voice in council?"

Odin nodded gravely. "Even as Thor."

Leif's eyes swept over the crowd. Heimdallr was busy polishing a part of his golden armor; Freyr was fingering his newly restored sword with open delight; Fulla's face was beaming, and Lee had his hands clasped together over his head in a vote of triumph; even Thor seemed to be looking on with a brotherly acceptance. Then Leif turned to Frigg again, and all the life seemed to go out of the company, leaving it in his mind as a picture of open and obvious hopelessness.

"Then I demand to be heard," Leif said.

The Alfadur shrugged and stepped back to his seat. "Speak then, Leif."

Leif felt like a fool at the attention focused on him; well, he'd never enjoyed making speeches, though he'd made enough at farmers' meetings. Loki could have made a better one, but Leif could at least tell them what he thought.

"My ancestors had a lousy religion once," he began abruptly. "It was the gloomiest, most futile one ever created. For every major god, they had something evil to kill him—and the better the god, the worse his fate. To make it neater, they had those gods knowing what was to happen. But that was all right—those ancestors of mine were only rude barbarians. They could have a serpent to kill Thor, Surtr to kill Freyr, Garm to kill Tyr, the Wolf against Odin, and a general burning of the universe by Surtr after evil had won.

"But then I was brought here to find that they got those notions from you—after you'd had thousands of years to live and learn better! You're still swallowing the same hog-wash today—even when you have already seen half of the predictions turn out to be a pack of has-been lies. You still think that the Norns—who couldn't even predict the sleep—are infallible. They were right about so-and-so, weren't they? The idea that *you made it come true* by believing every word they put out never entered your heads.

"Or take Frigg. Once, in trying to show off how well she could protect her mama's boy Balder, she got him killed. So now she sits here, staring at the sun and hating every man, doing nothing to help anyone but herself. But she gets away with it because she told you she knows all the future— though she can't tell it to you. That's the line little kids tell when they haven't studied their lessons: 'I know but I won't tell!' The truth is, she couldn't even tell you how Thor will avoid death from the Serpent's venom!"

Odin was looking at his wife now with a speculative doubt in his eye, and there was iron firmness in his voice. "Speak, Frigg!"

She snarled at Leif. "No one can tell that, since Thor dies by the venom. Tradition and my foreknowledge say it!"

"And both are liars," Leif told her flatly. "The dwarfs have made a plastic sheet that even hydrofluoric acid can't touch. In an inner suit of that, Thor can swim in the venom and laugh at you—as he *will* live through it. And what of all that bunk about Vali and Vidarr living beyond the Ragnarok to found a new world? Am I greater than your whole world, that I can upset your fixed future?"

Some of the gods muttered at that, but Leif went on, noticing it only out of a corner of his mind. "When I was brought here, I may have been a coward, as I was accused. But I wouldn't have sat around a witches' cauldron with a bunch of old women, being scared to death by fairy tales. I'm one of you now, and it's my future, by your own choice. So—*do you really want to win this war? Because you can.*"

Odin had been saying something to Frigg, and the god waited until she stepped down with blanched face and unbelieving eyes and began moving woodenly off. Then he turned back to Leif. "How?"

"Forget your traditions—stop waiting for the giants to bring the war to you. Use the courage all of you have individually, and take the weapons I have made against the giants, before they can organize. Wipe out *their* leaders while their traditions keep them helpless! "

Thor's bellow seconded it; it was a minor miracle that he should have been first to agree to breaking tradition, and for a moment, Leif dared to hope. Loki and Freyr joined. Odin nodded slowly. "I say this is a weighty thing, Leif, too great for one alone to decide. Those who would join in Leif's plan, stand to my right. Those who would await the Gjallar-Horn, choose my left."

Leif stared incredulously. Beside him, to the right of the throne, stepped Loki, Freyr, Fulla, Odin and Ullr. But the rest—even Heimdallr—stuck to tradition and moved to the left with the others.

They were to wait like sitting ducks for the giants to choose the time and make the attack.

CHAPTER XV

Leif shrugged, letting the hot spirit that had prompted the appeal die out, and went back to stand before Odin's seat. "All right, then, I suppose Thor and I might as well help you to Mimir's well. It's as good as anything else we can do."

Odin smiled faintly and shook his head, motioning Leif back. "My son, traditions here are things beyond reason. Yours, too, from what I have seen—though you count them as logic and ours as things to be put aside. For that logic of yours, and the thoughts you have given me, I like you—as I've liked Loki in spite of all the traditions against him. Well, the others have won, but my mind still spins. Let Mimir's well go. I have enough for thought already. The giants are warned now, and will strike too soon. Fulla needs you more than I—go to your bride and the work that is needed."

He turned and moved away, leaving Leif blinking, while Loki chuckled in the background. Fulla was moving slowly toward the buildings, her eyes to the ground, as Leif caught up with her. She refused to meet his eyes.

"Well?" he asked at last.

"The Alfadur had no business…Perhaps I said things while you were burned from Niflheim, but…Maybe I even said I needed you." She shook off his hand as he caught her arm. "But Leif, I know your heart isn't with Asgard. I know you mean to use Odin's boon to return to your earth. And since you have eaten of the apples for only a short time, and are hardly bound to your godhood, you can return, though it may be hard at first. I thought there was still a little time until then—until the Ragnarok; we have waited so long that it seems sometimes it can never come. I should have known that the Time is near, and that your words were only to soothe me while the giants had us."

He managed to pull her to him finally. "The words were what I felt in my heart, you precious little fool," he told her gravely. "You were the one who fought against me—and I was coming for you when the giant stole you. As for going back—if I can, I'll still want you with me—if you can give up all this to be just a simple farmer's wife. You'd have to pretend to be just a woman—not a goddess, of course."

"It wouldn't be pretense. My powers would fade there, and I *would* be only a woman. Odin, his true sons, and Loki are the only ones who can move freely without loss between the worlds."

"Oh." His hands began to drop from her shoulders.

She pressed them back. "Do you think that matters to me? Have I ever used any powers, other than when I revived you and the twining occurred? I'd go with you if I turned into a giantess! But it would never do. I've eaten the apples too long, and without them I'd grow old on Earth and die as a hideous hag. And you'd still be in your prime."

"We could take our share of the apples and keep them in the deep freeze…

"A few apples last all Asgard a thousand of your years, Leif…There are never more than a few. But on earth, all of them would be less than enough for one of us for a single decade! If we could take even one…"

She threw off the mood and drew his head down to her. "But we still have a few weeks before Ragnarok, Leif."

He looked down at her, comparing her to the girls he'd known, and even the dreams he'd had when he was very young and naive. He could see the smirks on the faces of Gefjun and the other goddesses, and he knew he should refuse for her sake. Instead, he smiled at her. "A few weeks can be a long time, my beloved."

It made her happy, apparently, as he had meant. But he knew that they would be short weeks—weeks driven and harried away from them by the rush to be ready for Ragnarok. The gods were hopelessly out-numbered, the einherjar almost useless. The giants would have all the advantage of knowing the time, and the Aesir would probably be defeated in advance by their own sense of inevitable defeat. There would be little time for love in the desperate days of trying to find ways to cancel out all the factors.

If the miracle of victory for the gods occurred, Leif had practically an eternity of life in a tradition-bound world where there was nothing to do but turn Earth into a vassal peasant world, subject to the whims of the gods. If they lost, Leif wouldn't have much knowledge of it, but the giants would wrack and raze earth with fire and destruction.

It was just a question of time before one of the two alternatives must be thrown at him. He wondered idly how much time and then dismissed the thought to clasp Fulla tighter.

* * * *

Then one morning a month later, when Leif and Fulla were together, something that sounded like all the klaxons invented went wailing and keening through the air. Fulla paled, terror running into her eyes. "Heimdallr blows the Gjallar-Horn! The giants are at Vigridr!"

Leif considered the fact that Ragnarok had begun. Now, as Leif Svensen, his duty was in the shops, to wait for the results. But as Leif Odinsson, his place was to the fore-oh. He began buckling on his armor, with Fulla's help. Finished, he blinked as she came out with a suit of mail, motioning for him to help her into it.

She met his eyes firmly. "I'm fighting. Do you think I care what happens if you don't come back to me, Leif?"

He knew he should protest, according to Earth traditions, but he felt no desire to do so. If she wanted to be in the battle, that was right for her. He helped her quietly, and went out through the workshop entrance, where the worried dwarfs tried to yell encouragement after him. The work there was done, as best it could be. Leif moved toward the stables, seeing no other god near them, still trying to realize that the day of doom had struck. But the fear he expected refused to come. He was only conscious of a vague relief that the waiting was over.

Lee caught up to him, swung around for a better look, and grinned. "You've got it, son. All of it. I always knew you'd make a better hero than I do, and by Ymir, I was right. You'll be around after this is over—nothing can kill a man when he's got as much of it as you do."

"I'm not scared, if that's what you mean, Lee. But I'm still not one of your fighting men. I'm not looking forward to this for the thrill of it, or laughing about it."

"No—no, of course not." Lee frowned in thought. "You don't have to, I guess. You can go in cold and deadly serious, like Thor or Tyr. Look, my godly twin, d'you know what would happen if Loki or I quit pretending it was all just a joke or a thrill? We'd funk out! We don't dare take it seriously. It has to be a game to us. Damn it, if I don't get off this soap box, I *will* funk out! Wish me luck!"

He almost bumped into Fulla, chucked her under the chin, and was gone at a run toward Thor's group of einherjar, his voice taking on parade drill tones before he reached them.

Leif found the Valkyries busy saddling and cut through their chatter. "I'm guessing that nobody gave you orders, right? Well, what are you plans?"

Reginleif looked doubtful, still not used to his godhood. "To the battle, as always—to rescue the heroes…"

She fumbled, and Leif grinned wryly.

"Tradition, isn't it? To rescue the new heroes! Not this time, not by a damn sight! All right, get on the horses and go over to the shop of the dwarfs. Sudri and his boys are ready, and they'll load you up with grenades and tell you where to haul and dump them."

"I won't take orders from the dwarfs," Reginleif began. Leif Svensen cut her off. "You mean you don't like to take such orders. But you'll do it, or I'll give your horses to those same dwarfs and send you to live with them. Now get going! Fulla, you and Hoof-Tosser work together well enough, and Gna doesn't know anything about this business. Take him and a few of these girls. They can lug the small U-235 bombs up to Bifrost, where you can carry them over to the trails in Muspelheim and Jotunheim. You know what to do?"

She repeated the plans they had discussed. Under the stupid tradition, he hadn't been able to take precautions in advance, but he could cut off most of the reinforcements and prevent their getting through from the giant worlds by dropping the bombs on them where they were massed outside the entrance to Vigridr. The stone dwarfs had modified the time element in the detonators to give the bomb carriers a chance to escape.

Leif nodded approval as he heard her repeat the plans. "Good. Hoof-Tosser is the only horse that can get off the ground, except over Earth, and probably the only one strong enough to carry a bomb across even these easy borders. Take care of yourself, and don't get too low."

She matched his mood by avoiding all show of emotions. He left as he saw her begin to give the Valkyries their orders. Loki and Thor were standing together, and he approached them, noticing that the black-bearded god was wearing his plastic under armor properly. "How bad is it?" Loki gestured toward Leif's mirror, and they all moved toward the wall, where they could watch Asgard and examine Vigridr through the barrier. Sometimes Leif almost forgot that the little battle world lay across Bifrost in another dimensional twist, since it lay so close. Passage to it was so easy that the pigs had to be chased back regularly from it, and even the oldest heroes had no trouble.

Odin and Freyr had already assembled their troops at the end of the battlefield nearest Asgard, and Tyr was coming through now with his. Vigridr field was better than a hundred miles on a side, taking up most of the largest land mass of the tiny world. Lee Svensen came moving through then with the left wing of Thor's band—the strongest and smartest of the heroes, on the whole. As Leif watched, he saw the Valkyries begin to move down, dragging wooden sleds filled with grenades behind them, in addition to those belted to the heroes.

CHAPTER XVI

There was a mist over the field, and at first Leif could make out nothing of the giants. When it began to clear, he groaned at what he could see. The forces of the Aesir seemed lost in a tiny corner of the field, compared to the seemingly endless expanse of giant strength. And only the pick of the monsters were there—none less than thirty feet in height, and one whole company running to nearly twice that. They were armed with everything from swords through pikes to maces—and the last looked the most dangerous. But he could see no sign of bows and arrows, or of the cement-tamper gadget he'd have dreamed up if he had wanted to go around killing off the Aesir forces from their height. It had seemed so obvious to Leif that he had half expected to see it in use—though he knew that what was obvious was actually so only in a milieu such as his own.

"It looks worse than it is," Loki said. "Vigridr has a gravity only about a quarter normal, and we're more agile. But as you may have noticed, Jotunheim has even less, and the frost giants feel too heavy for comfort, while the fire giants are used to nearly three times our gravity. They feel themselves so light that they have to remember not to use their full strength, and it slows them up."

Asgard would need the advantage, and it might not be enough, Leif decided. "How'd so many get there, anyhow?" Heimdallr came up and caught the question, buckling on the plainest, dirtiest, dullest and heaviest armor Leif had yet seen, and swinging a sword that seemed designed for two men. There was a curious drive to his voice, totally unlike the usual drawl he affected. "My fault, brother. While I watched the main trails for the march to begin, these were coming in on small trails, a few at a time, hiding in the grasses, and waiting for this day. You were right—we should have struck them first. Well, good luck among them."

Leif felt the three clips in his pouch. All his cartridges had been carefully reloaded by the dwarfs—a job which was barely within their skill. Thus, the powder was poorer than before, but it would have to do. He checked the grenades at his side and loosened the buckle of his new sword. He'd had Sudri alloy and forge it from the toughest formula he could find on Earth. It was thin and light, but this sword's cutting edge could shear through normal steel as if it were paper. He'd imitated Freyr's sword as best he could, and tried to sell the idea to the others. But they preferred the familiar, just as they distrusted this thin, tough armor Leif had had forged. They were used to mail, and he couldn't convince them that his type of armor spread the shock better. But many of them were carrying the little polished shields that could be used horizontally, to signal reflections of any sudden movement above the wearer, giving almost a full circle of vision against the giants.

He started to climb into Thor's chariot, but stopped at a sudden shout that went up from the Aesir. "Naglfar!"

Something was coming through from Jotunheim. The thing was having difficulty, and none of it emerged clearly, but it looked like an immense ship. Then he could see that it was a huge mobile fort, equipped with everything from a great ram to ballistas. It rolled on huge wheels, powered by a multi-legged monster of incredible size. The thing seemed ugly enough to wipe out half the Aesir by itself. At the moment, it seemed unable to work through into Vigridr. It was beginning to draw back, probably to look for a better place. But once it got through…

He saw Fulla in the distance, directing some work of the dwarfs, and opened his mouth in a scream that seemed to sear his throat. To his surprise, Hoof-Tosser echoed it and took off like a shot, carrying Fulla with him. Leif began shouting orders as soon as she was near, and she waved assent and swung back to the dwarfs.

Loki's expression was curious now, and the god had apparently forgotten the monster fort. "Your powers are developing early, Leif Odinsson—too early. Few of the gods even, and no mortal, can use the Summons. I'm not sure I like it."

"I'm less sure that I like surprises," Leif told him. "Why wasn't I told about that fort of the giants in time to do something in advance?"

Thor rumbled unhappily. "With Hrymr dead, there seemed no danger, brother. He was supposed to drive it and no other giant had the skill. And that may have caused them to delay this long, while they trained one of his sons."

Naglfar had come up against Bifrost at another place, apparently. At least the size of the color ripples suggested something of that size. It would be pushing through in another minute.

Fulla went racing by overhead, with Hoof-Tosser fleeing from Jotunheim like a soul released from Niflheim. Then Bifrost seemed to buckle and develop diffraction patterns. For a few seconds, the outline of Naglfar seemed etched out of blinding light against the colors. The outline crumpled like a paper toy and something beat against the sky like a drummer hitting skin. The subsonic waves shook the ground, to fade with the glaring lights.

Even Thor's voice sounded like a faint whisper after that. "Ymir! What was that?"

"U-235," Leif answered, and waved up to Fulla. One of the bombs he'd ordered placed near each main assembly spot in Jotunheim had already proved its worth. But it had been a close call.

Thor was ready now, and Leif waved at Loki, who would be the messenger, since his skill at sleight could serve as enough disguise to make him pass unnoticed during the rage of the battle. Thor yelled at the goats and they went slipping along the edge of Bifrost, setting a pace the einherjar could follow. Leif looked at the heroes with mixed contempt and pity. They were going into something that was beyond their imagining, but most of them didn't have enough of the life-force left to realize this was more than a routine day. And those with almost no life-force in their elf-shaped flesh had been held for reserves; it would be a sorry day if they were needed.

"I've had no training in this, Thor," Leif commented. "I won't be much help to you."

"Training!" Thor spat over the side of the chariot. "It takes another virtue, Leif. I'm glad to have you with me, and if the Serpent gets me, it will be good to know you're here to lead my band. Ho! They're moving."

Odin's band had started, and the distant figure of Odin could be seen in his gold helmet, holding what seemed to be a spear. Leif grinned, glad of the last-minute inspiration that had made him change the spear to a bazooka and furnish Odin with a load of trick shells for it. It had taxed the abilities of the dwarfs, but they had succeeded.

Out of the giant group a band moved forward, headed by something out of deepest nightmare. "Fenris Wolf, the Gaping Wolf," Thor said, but Leif had already guessed it. It looked a little like a wolf, though it rose to a height of forty feet at the shoulders and had teeth five feet long, dripping a raw green fire of radioactivity. He shuddered, looking for the other monsters. He saw a great creature, looped into coils, projecting a head larger than a twenty-foot boat; but it wasn't a true serpent, since it sprouted hundreds of short, stumpy legs and bore a dozen arms, all loaded with weapons. The third horror was harder to see—something that seemed to flame and blaze in outlines that the eyes refused to admit. That must be the dog Garm.

He shuddered again. Somewhere in his mind, a dim memory of things like that in Niflheim tried to clarify itself. Thor nodded, as if reading his mind. "The fire giants, being more terrible than the ones from Jotunheim, dragged these creatures from Niflheim long and long ago—so long that the giants now believe Fenris Wolf is the father of them all. They are dreadful opponents."

They were more than that, and Leif's admiration for Tyr increased as he watched the god drive his force against the thing called Garm. Then Thor yelled, and his own band was moving toward the Serpent. Thor handed the reins to Leif, checked his hammer, gloves and belt, and dropped over the side, running forward. The giants behind the Serpent came forward with a rush.

Leif's eyes dropped to the long blades projecting from the axles of the chariot, and he hoped the accounts he'd read of the Egyptian use of them would prove true. It had been another last-minute idea. He whooped at the goats and let them go all out, fairly sure that their armor, built like his own, could withstand the giant weapons.

At the last moment he swerved, dug deeper into the protective front of the chariot, and shaved down the side of the giant ranks. There was a series of grinding jolts to the chariot motion now, and a howling above that threatened to break his eardrums. He came to the end of the rank of giants, stealing a quick look back. It seemed impossible that so many giants could have been robbed of their legs in that one brief passage. The blades at the sides really worked, and the old Egyptians had been smart boys. Of course, having the pulling power of Thor's goats in front helped, as did better steel for the blades.

The giants were swinging toward him now, though, and he cut around their rear, barely shaving through them as they tried to close up. This time, while they were swinging to face him, he drove down the other flank, catching their legs from the rear before they could dodge or face him. He sprang to his feet and began tossing grenades into their ranks. He shook his head at the mental picture he had of himself, wondering how he could take all this with the same attitude as butchering time on the farm.

The giants lacked discipline—but that was nothing compared to the lack showing among the einherjar. Some of them were standing off at the side, happily swinging away at each other, as if they were back practicing in Asgard! Leif let out a yelp and was in among them, as close as he dared come in the chariot, trying to bring order out of their behavior. He indicated the grenades, and they began picking them up and throwing them toward the giants. Half didn't explode, for want of will, but those that worked helped considerably. Leif swung back.

A grenade from his own einherjar promptly hit the back of the chariot, knocking one wheel to splinters!

CHAPTER XVII

Pieces of wheel and chariot were flying through the air as Leif jumped. He landed with a jolt that shook his whole body, but he seemed to be unharmed, except for minor cuts and bruises. The goats had also come through without injury, but the chariot was a total wreck. Cursing the imbecility of heroes, Leif Svensen began unhitching the animals. At a swat from the side of his hand, they went trotting off toward Asgard and the stables.

Fulla yelled from high overhead, and Leif waved up to show that he was still safe. She dropped a rain of grenades into the ranks of the giants near him and went galloping back for more. As their only air force, she was proving to be the Aesir's best warrior, and reasonably safe in addition. Leif struck off at a lope that covered some twenty miles an hour in the reduced gravity, refilling his belt with grenades that had not exploded and avoiding the thickest clumpings of the giants.

It was necessary to stick somewhere near the einherjar and to keep them from straying. He found himself suddenly bottled along with one of the heroes. Leif's grenades had been exhausted, and now there was no opening in the giant ranks. He motioned to the hero, and they went leaping ahead together, ducking among the grouped giant legs, moving where it was almost impossible for a spear to be poked at him. He was using his sword to maim rather than kill, since a wounded giant caused more confusion than a dead one. Beside him, the hero was happily taking care of those that Leif missed, with a co-operation that was unusual for one of the einherjar. Then Leif came to an unexpected group of grenades that some Valkyr had dropped. The giants wanted no part of the explosions; they began giving ground at once. One spotted a grenade on the ground, scooped it up and tossed it at Leif, but the detonators were not tuned to giant minds. He caught it and fired it back—to remove the last of the nearby giants.

The hero grunted amicably. "We fight now, huh?"

Leif strangled over the words, but managed to keep his voice calm as he sent the hero off after more giants in the distance. Still, if they had all been like that one, it wouldn't be so bad. He counted over a score of dead giants and sped down the field, wondering if there was anything to Lee's theory that a man who was both calculating and unafraid couldn't be killed in battle. It should make a good condition for survival, unlike the heady dreams of excitement he had felt as a child. Leif Svensen had wanted to seek grails, and he'd envied every man who found adventure or new worlds to conquer. For a time, he had envied Lee most of all. Now, in a situation that no story book would have covered, he had little time and less desire for anything beyond survival.

He leaped ten feet into the air over a dead giant and ran on toward what was left of his group of einherjar.

"Ho, Leif!" It was Thor, apparently wading through giants, his hammer a steady drumming that left a string of broken giant heads. With his other hand, he was swinging a big battle axe. Leif saw the giants closing around him like cornered rats making a last desperate bid, and went in from the outside, scattering them again, to give Thor room for his hammer work. Actually, it wasn't too much different— except for the reversal of roles—from his experience in digging real rats out of a granary foundation. Try as he would, he hadn't been able to hit one of them, though Rex had been killing them easily. They had been much too small and active for Leif, as he was now for the giants.

"Garm got Tyr," Thor announced sadly, swinging the axe over Leif's head to chop off part of a giant. He reached out for the returning hammer, spotted a giant leg temptingly near, and swiveled on his hip to lock a leg into that of the giant. The giant tripped and fell where Leif could take care of him. "Though Garm died after the victory from the damage Tyr's one arm had done. And you've proved to be a better prophet than Frigg or the Norns, since I've killed the Midgard Serpent and Odin has a tooth of Fenris Wolf as a trophy. Where is Lee? "

Leif shook his head and backed against Thor as three of the giants came charging at them. He barely caught the spear on the slant of his shield, deflecting it without trying to stop it. Even then, it sent a surge of pain up his arm. He had noticed that it was getting harder to dodge and save himself, as the giants grew accustomed to Vigridr and the fighting style of the gods. And he was having to watch himself, to make sure that his success didn't make him careless. Thor did his fighting by pure conditioned reflex action, but Leif wasn't good enough to grow over-confident safely.

From the edge of the field, there was a piercing hail, and a half dozen of the Valkyries came riding toward them, armed heavily with grenades, and intent on finding giants for targets. For a time, they turned the tide back to a steady condition of giant killing, rather than war, and the giants began to retreat. Some of the better einherjar worked more smoothly with the women, and there were knots that seemed to be operating with almost full efficiency. The normal einherjar remained more of menace than a help, however; the fighters were always in danger of getting a grenade in the back from one of their own men.

Thor found a lull in the action and began pulling out hunks of his plastic under-armor, shaking sweat from his body with it. Leif tried to help him, so they could get back into the fight sooner. Most of the plastic came out through the openings in the armor. They were pulling the last away when Loki seemed to materialize out of nothing before them.

Both Thor and Lee bombarded him with questions, but there was still no good way of estimating the battle from down on the field. Loki had been up with Fulla, getting a better look at things, and he didn't seem happy about it.

"Lee's collected five heroes who seem to have some sense, and he's got Gefjun and a couple other Asynjur freighting supplies. He's doing more damage to the giants than the leader of any group. And we're all doing miracles—thanks to the grenades and the bombs that killed off the giant reserves. But we're still losing—and badly. They hold most of the field, except around the entrance to Asgard, and they're closing in there. Even if every hero kills twenty of them, they can beat us. We're already doing our best, too. The women are fighting as hard as the men, letting the dwarfs take over all supply work. Sudri and a group of his people are even joining in the fighting."

Thor scowled in surprise and doubt. "What can a dwarf do? You exaggerate, Loki."

Loki pointed to a section of the field not too distant. "See for yourself."

Four of the squat little figures were banded together, tossing grenades as they drove a few giants back. One was suddenly caught in the clutch of a giant hand. Leif saw that it was Sudri, and groaned, but a second later the dwarf dropped back, spitting, while the big hand dropped beside him. He darted forward and grabbed a leg of another monster, his mouth working rapidly, before an eddy of battle cut off the sight.

There was a warning cry from Loki, and Leif had a brief glimpse of something flickering in the reflection on his shield. He leaped fifteen feet sideways, just as a heavy mace thwacked down beside him, the sharp spikes clanging against his armor and opening six inches of skin along his leg. Half attention was dangerous here! While the gods had been talking, a band of giants had sneaked up on them with a silence which seemed impossible to the clumsy creatures.

Loki and Leif set to work together, while Thor's hammer and axe began a giant dirge. A grenade from a wandering hero went off against the midsection of one monster, throwing Leif to his knees and killing the hero in the concussion. There were no unbruised places on his body, it seemed—but he also seemed to bear a charmed life, and was back in the fight almost at once. A few minutes later, Loki was cutting the ugly throat of the last enemy near them.

But now, even Leif could see that the battle was being lost by Asgard. The giants were advancing slowly. At first, they had been cautious of the heroes, but now that fear seemed to be gone, leaving them free to concentrate on their real enemies. Size and number were both on their side. "How much longer can we hold out?" Leif asked Loki. "Perhaps two hours, but certainly no more."

"And where's Odin?"

He headed in the direction Loki had pointed, keeping his eyes open for one of the dwarfs. By good luck, he found Sudri a few minutes later. The dwarf was running back for more grenades, but swung around with obvious delight at finding Leif still whole.

Leif Svensen had no time for greetings. "Can you build rails out over Vigridr—the higher the better—through Bifrost from Asgard? I want a place to move in a score of bombs over the field, too high for the giants to reach."

"Sure, boss Leif. Stuff won't weigh much here, and that part of Bifrost is thin. Brace the platforms from Asgard. You want it done now?"

"On the double, Sudri," Leif ordered, and headed for the section where Odin was supposed to be, avoiding giants as best he could. It was still odd to be able to run a mile in two minutes, but a welcome thing now. He found Odin presently, mixed into the thick of things, with a couple of the Valkyries, a hero, and a dwarf—the strangest mixture Leif had seen, but a surprisingly effective one. The giants near them were already beginning to retreat by the time Leif reached the group and began helping to clean up the last ones.

Odin looked good now, more vigorous and youthful than Leif had seen him before; but the worry in his eye showed that Loki had been in touch with him. Leif wasted no time on preliminaries. "Can you order a complete retreat and make it work?"

The Alfadur's face clouded in suspicion, but the old head finally nodded doubtfully. Leif began explaining his plan, bracing himself as he came to what he most hated about it. The reserve einherjar were certainly of no use, even to themselves. They were no more alive than the weapons they carried. But because the elf-shapings had once housed something—the complex life patterns of real men, whether that was the stuff of souls or of something as synthetic as the outer bodies—it bothered him to demand their coldblooded sacrifice. And he knew that Odin was fond of all his heroes.

Odin had hated the knowledge that the heroes killed here in Vigridr were lost forever. There was no way of restoring them on this little world, and carrying them back through Bifrost would do something, apparently, that would also prevent restoration. But at least their deaths had seemed necessary and honorable; even Leif could see little honor in the betrayal that was needed now.

The Alfadur took it on his own conscience, adding the matter to all the worries that had driven him through millennia. When it was clear there was no other solution, he nodded at the harsh laws of military necessity.

"As you have said, Leif, there are many of the einherjar who are less than beasts, knowing neither pleasure nor pain," he conceded. "This is an ill thing, and if those will suffice, you have my permission. Go back and do whatever is needful. Here, we shall try to organize for the bitter retreat. And hasten—the time is less than even Loki thought."

Leif headed for Bifrost, still trying to avoid further fighting now. There was no time to spare for individual giant killing. He ducked around a huge corpse, leaped over a pile of squashed einherjar where a giant had trapped and trampled them, and dived rapidly under the falling sword of a smaller giant. Then he was in a clearer space, and his eyes began a frantic search for Fulla or Hoof-Tosser. She caught the signal of the light reflections from his shield and came plummeting down on Hoof-Tosser, to touch the ground lightly and dart up again as soon as Leif could pull himself up behind her.

Her hand squeezed hard on his wrist, but she made no comment, and he was too exhausted to waste words. He found a remaining scrap of the share of apple all had been given and swallowed it as they flashed through Bifrost. It helped, though there was too little of it. He was able to jump briskly from the horse and move quickly to the workshops.

The dwarfs were almost finished with the crude platform and rails that ran from the shops to the top of the wall and then out through Bifrost. Leif moved out on it, to the edge of the platform beyond the edge of Vigridr, perhaps two hundred feet above the ground and two hundred square feet in area. The bracing back to the wall on Asgard had already been completed, and the first sled with its load was dragged up the greased rails as Leif watched. He made a few suggestions, and moved back to Asgard.

It was amazing how time was slipping away. Loki was waiting for him, with Heimdallr at his side, when Leif stepped from the wall. The vain god was now blood-spattered and filthy, almost unrecognizable, but the horn in his hand still sparkled like a precious jewel. "I'm to sound retreat when you're ready," he announced. "But who's to lead the sacrificial einherjar?"

Leif frowned, shaking the cobwebs from his brain. Of course there had to be a leader for the heroes, since they couldn't even remember orders more than a minute or two, unless they could simply ape the acts of a god in front of them. They needed only brains enough to keep the giants from realizing it was retreat and not mere replacement for perhaps five minutes, but that was beyond their ability. He'd overlooked that angle.

Now he faced it, and the solution was obvious. "All right. It was my idea, so I'll lead."

"Don't be a fool," Loki snapped. "It means death."

"It means the same death to anyone else," Leif pointed out. "I can't ask someone else to die in my place."

Fulla made a low moaning sound in her throat and braced herself against Hoof-Tosser. There was an appeal in her eyes, but she nodded reluctantly as he faced her. Maybe it was better this way, he thought. They'd had a month together, which was more than they had expected; and once Ragnarok was over, he could only be a source of trouble to her.

From a watching dwarf, the signal that Odin was ready was relayed back to Leif, and he nodded for Heimdallr to sound retreat. The Gjallar-Horn that could sound through all the worlds came up, wailing as if ten thousand banshees were attending the wake of the last idshee in the universe. Heimdallr dropped the horn at last and stretched out his hand. Leif reached out to accept the gesture.

The hand doubled into a fist that shoved suddenly against his chest. Something caught behind his knees, and he went sailing over the kneeling figure of Loki—a victim of a trick older than even the traditions of Asgard!

CHAPTER XVIII

He sprang to his feet almost instantly, but Heimdallr was running toward the apathetic ranks of the oldest heroes, waving them forward. They started mechanically into Bifrost, with Heimdallr at the front.

"You never know about him," Loki muttered. "But in a way, he was right. You did your job here, and more. He made a mistake earlier in not spotting the first giants who drifted into Vigridr. Now he has to make up for it."

Fulla was with them as Leif and Loki stepped along the rails into Vigridr again, watching the change-over. Odin had somehow managed to marshal his forces into a thin strip before the entrance, and even to force the giants back temporarily. Now Heimdallr broke through Bifrost, his horn wailing, and went boring ahead, drawing his ranks through the others. Leif could see that he was, indeed, the man for the job now. Heimdallr did it with a flair that somehow made every faded hero a temporary extension of himself, and he got them through undivided and even into some kind of action against the giants. It was superb leadership, with almost nothing to lead.

Odin raised his spear. Gods, Valkyries, dwarfs, and the heroes who had been intelligent enough to obey orders pelted for Bifrost. The giants hesitated, uncertain about the strange maneuver; it was no part of the traditional battle plan, and they had seen too many new things prove dangerous. They even gave ground a little before Heimdallr's rush. Then they began a forward movement again, but still cautiously.

There was no sign of Lee that Leif could see. The other Svensen might have been too tightly knit into the main group to be seen, or he might have already been a victim of his own bravery, as Heimdallr seemed likely to be within a few minutes.

Leif felt something touch his arm and turned to see Hoof-Tosser delicately stepping along the rails, rubbing his nuzzle against Leif. Apparently, the horse had gotten tired of being alone—or perhaps curious about the battle, since he seemed to understand more than any horse could. Leif jerked out of his mental fog abruptly and grabbed the reins to pull the horse forward onto the platform. There were still a few grenades on the saddle—enough, perhaps. He vaulted into place and was urging Hoof-Tosser into the air in a split second.

At first, there seemed to be no sign of Heimdallr, until a toppling giant showed the god briefly. Leif urged Hoof-Tosser down, swinging his sword toward a giant neck. The horse wheeled at once, making a perfect target of another giant, and the sword bit deeply again. For a moment, there was a clear space.

Heimdallr was not fool enough to argue; the god leaped up, lifting his arm, and Leif caught it, yelling for Hoof-Tosser to get back to Asgard.

The weight of the god and armor was too much for Leif to heave up to the saddle, and Hoof-Tosser's legs threatened to send Heimdallr flying into space. Yet somehow the legs managed to miss him, and he caught a stirrup with his other hand and gradually floundered up behind Leif. Below, the last of the forces of Asgard were off the field, and the giants had finally realized something was wrong. They were pelting across the field in a mass charge, disregarding the hopeless einherjar. Heimdallr grabbed for the grenades and tossed them back, but there was no time to see the results.

Leif yelled to the dwarfs as Hoof-Tosser leaped through Bifrost and dropped to the cave entrance beside Loki and Fulla.

The dwarfs were into Vigridr and darting back by the time Leif and Heimdallr had dismounted. Loki pulled the dimensional mirror from his pouch. Leif knocked it from his hand, just as a stabbing beam of radiance leaped from it and lanced across the ground, searing the grass instantly.

Even in Asgard, the shock wave shook the ground, and Bifrost became visible for miles of its length, arching and leaping in rainbow fire. But thin as it was here, the dimensional twists of Bifrost held back the major shock and lethal radiations. Twenty of the biggest U-235 bombs going off together represented a violence greater than the worst legends could match. In the tiny world of Vigridr, there was no room for such fury. Even the crust of the planet must be cracking under it. When the fury faded a little, Leif picked up the mirror. There was no evidence of life now on Vigridr. It was clothed only with decaying radiance, and the giants were no longer a danger to Asgard.

Leif found Odin and Thor later. The two were still unsure of this victory that had replaced certain doom. Leif was dead inside with reaction from the flux of emotions he'd never known he was experiencing, but something stirred briefly as he sensed the Alfadur's mood. The old god stood looking down at Asgard from a low hillock, only half seeing it.

"Five gods, four goddesses, a score of my Valkyries, and all but a handful of the einherjar are gone. Even nine of the dwarfs. Let Sudri have a seat on the council as an equal for this day's work, and add his losses to ours. Gna is dead, and she has left Hoof-Tosser to you, Leif. Frigg has killed herself, since her prophecy has failed. Tyr and Ullr are no more. It is a heavy price. Yet Asgard is saved, and I have still three mighty sons beside me. My heart is full." Odin's dirge and eulogy ended, and he stood there silently for another minute. Then he sighed and faced the others, his expression almost normal again. "Now we must reckon accounts at Yggdrasil."

He moved away. The ravens swooped down to his shoulder and the two grey old wolves came up to trot beside him. Leif, Fulla, Thor, Loki and Heimdallr watched until he was almost gone from sight, and even Loki had nothing to say.

Thor spoke first, dropping an oddly gentle hand on Leif's shoulder. "Leif, your brother Lee is safe and will join us at the council. He was wounded badly, but Gefjun found him and dragged him out at the last moment. She's tending him now. Heimdallr, are you coming?"

"I'm coming," the fair god said. He moved off with Thor, but his words drifted back. "Thor, that trick of building a structure across Bifrost from the wall is worth seeing first. I've studied it, and it's a better trick than it seems. With it, we can build through to Midgard, to conquer and to hold it easily!"

Leif Svensen had started forward with them, but now he stopped, frozen by the picture of Earth being ravaged by his own devices. In the aftermath of Ragnarok, he'd almost forgotten the inevitable sequel to it, but now reality swooped back. He'd saved Asgard—but left Earth completely at the mercy of the gods!

"I've got to go back," he decided. "Fulla, it will be hell without you, but I can't betray my world—not even for you."

She made no reply, but her hand tightened on his.

Loki snorted. "Going back won't save anything! Your skills are already familiar there, Leif. Don't be a fool!"

All of Leif's half-formed plans churned in his head now, but he had never had time to develop them. "I still have a boon from Odin due me," he said, trying to make it convincing to himself. "If I demand that the Aesir give up their plans against Earth…"

"You'd fail. Leif, do you think a priest of one of your faiths would give up his right to convert others? He might give you even the altar and every treasure of his temple—but not his duty to what he considers lost souls! Odin might give you a truce for a generation, perhaps—but even he couldn't enforce it. Kings may relinquish their thrones, but they don't abdicate unless they have already lost the power to hold. I'll help you, Leif—but not in madness!"

He stared at Leif for a moment, waiting for some response, but seeing none. Then he shrugged and moved away toward Yggdrasil.

Leif and Fulla followed more slowly along a path that had too many memories for them. Her hand was still tightly clasped in his. Then she halted. "Take me with you, Leif."

"I can't," he told her. "It's easy to think of now. But I couldn't watch you grow old and wither, and know I was responsible. You've told me yourself that you couldn't adapt to Earth, Fulla."

She nodded faintly, and pulled her hand free. "Then let me leave you here, before I break. I can't stay while you're torn from me by slow inches, Leif."

She came into his arms for one kiss, drew back and managed to smile at him. Then she moved up the trail without looking back.

He moved up the trail toward Yggdrasil alone, his thoughts and emotions churning on into inevitability.

The Aesir were all assembled when he arrived. He saw Lee first, standing beside Gefjun. There was an ugly scar across Lee's chest, but the rapid healing customary in Asgard had proceeded so far that no sign of weakness remained. He began running forward with a beaming face as he spotted Leif.

Then the expression changed to surprise as he stared at Leif. "What's eating you, son?"

"I'm going back to Earth. Are you coming with me, Lee?" Lee's laugh was automatic. "Well, I suppose it'll be pretty dull around here with no war. And Gefjun's getting ideas." The laughter faded as he studied his brother, and he frowned, shaking his head as if amazed at himself. "But…No, damn it. Leif, I guess I fit here better than I ever did back there. And I've already sort of promised her…Unless you need me, son?"

"Go back to your goddess," Leif told him. He forced a smile to his lips and clapped Lee lightly on the back. He was getting used to the idea of going it alone, it seemed. Anyhow, it was his responsibility, not Lee's. He saw that Gefjun was carrying the chest of apples, and knew there was no point in looking for Fulla in the crowd. He moved toward Odin's throne.

The business going on stopped as the Aesir spotted him. Odin came to his feet, motioning toward the seat that Frigg had previously occupied. "My son Leif, it is time for you to take your rightful place with us here!"

"I've got a question and a boon first, Father Odin," Leif called back.

"Then speak. We have already promised you one request within the limit of our powers. You have earned the boon this day."

"The question first," Leif said. He saw Loki struggling through the throng toward him, but he had no intention of discussing things further. "Am I free to return to Earth— to Midgard? Or am I to be held here?"

Surprise mingled with a sharp disappointment on Odin's face, but the old head nodded gravely. "Leif, no son of Odin is a prisoner on any world! Your right to return as we thought you knew, has existed since first you were adopted here. It is our hope that you will remain—but no one shall detain you!"

Leif considered the fact that he could have gone at any time, but it didn't matter. After seeing the giants, he could never have deserted the Aesir until their battle was decided. Now, though, his obligation was to his own world, no matter what his feelings might be. Yet he still hesitated, considering and rechecking the only solution that he had finally found.

"Your request?" Odin prompted him.

"All right," Leif said at last. He lifted his voice for all to hear. "Let me take all the sacred apples back to Earth with me!"

It was the only possible answer. As Loki had said, the gods would never give up their claim to their ancestral planet. And while the loss of the apples would return them to sleep for another thousand years, it was only a delay. It was a truce that none could break until the sleep was finished, and then they could try to sack Earth, if they liked. By that time, Earth should be able to take care of herself, even if Bifrost remained open.

For a few seconds after his demand, there had been a stunned silence. Now suddenly it was shattered by a tumult of furious cries.

"Traitor!" The loudest bellow was that of the normally quiet Freyr. His superlative sword was out now, and the god was charging forward. "Slay the traitor!"

The shouting unified behind him, and the mob began moving purposefully, drawing their weapons. Days of waiting for doom, battle rage, broken prophecies and unexpected victory had left their nerves balanced on a sword edge, and now they snapped. "Niflheim! To Niflheim with Loki's cub!"

"Justice!" Thor's bellow sounded over all other voices, and his hammer split the air before the crowd in a screaming rush. "This is a judging place. Let judgment be made!"

For a moment, the crowd stopped and milled uncertainly as Thor's hammer sped back to his hand. But even he could not hold them all in check. Odin was pounding for order with his spear. Then Heimdallr lifted the Gjallar-Horn, just as the ravens darted from Odin's shoulders and headed for Leif and Loki.

The brazen clamor of Heimdallr's blast was like the thrust of a sea wave, driving all before it.

In the hush that followed, the raven landed on Leif's shoulder, beating its wings and croaking harshly. "Odin commands! Go at once to the workshops and remain until released!"

The shops were still too near, Leif felt. And he had no intention of waiting while they voted whether to kill him or send him to Niflheim. He lifted his head to call the summons for Hoof-Tosser. Then he caught sight of the single eye of Odin, fixed on him, fully open, commanding...

Leif's legs began moving under him against his will, heading for the workshops. He gave up resisting until he was out of sight of Yggdrasil, then fought for control. But it was useless. He saw Lee run up to join him, but could not even turn in greeting. Without faltering, his legs moved steadily onward, carrying him toward the shops.

CHAPTER XIX

Dusk was settling on Asgard when two figures approached the shops. Lee Svensen was pacing about, but Leif sat quietly smoking; he had tried to move twice, but the force of Odin's mental command was still in control. The figures drew nearer and turned into Thor and Odin. Now at last, Leif could feel the compulsion leave his legs, but he made no effort to rise.

Odin came up first, looking down at him, and the god's shoulders were slumped with fatigue. Gravely, he dropped a chest to the ground at Leif's feet. "The apples are all there, Leif, my son. So long as we rule here, no man or god may say that the word of Odin is an empty thing. The Aesir pay their debts."

The shock was greater to Leif than that of the crowd's reaction to his request. He had been expecting and planning for anything but this.

"I'm sorry, Father Odin," he said slowly, rising at last. Something in the grave old figure made the acknowledgment of relationship more than a formal salutation. "I had no wish to be another of the sons who have betrayed you…"

"Nor are you." Thor's voice was brusque and as low as it could ever be. "The shame lies with the Aesir, and Heimdallr has preached from Jotunheim to vanished Vanaheim and back until they know and regret their error. When a man or god betrays his roots, there is no honor in him— when he is true to them, nothing can make a traitor of him. By Ymir, once I saw the thought behind your request, I'd have chained you between Asgard and Niflheim if you had asked for less. The vote was unanimous. Take the apples, brother, and go back to Midgard with your conscience clear—as we shall sleep with ours."

Leif turned back into the caves, puzzling over it. Asgard would always be a place of surprises, and not the least of the amazing things was the length of Thor's speech.

Sudri was waiting with a mournful face. He accepted the automatic and put it away mechanically, nodding at his new instructions. His eyes brightened as Leif held out his hand in farewell, but tears kept falling down his ugly face, and he seemed to have no voice.

Outside again, Leif picked up the apples and turned to Odin. "Sudri can protect the entrances to Asgard while you sleep. The dwarfs know how to use the bombs and grenades. And I've told him how to care for the tree. He may even be able to develop more trees for you."

There seemed to be nothing else to say. He strapped the chest to his belt, feeling strange without the armor he'd gotten used to. Then he lifted his head and called. An answering nicker came at once, and Hoof-Tosser dropped down beside him, nuzzling him gently.

Odin dropped his hands on Leif's shoulders. "Wherever you are, you have the power to summon Hoof-Tosser to you—to carry you about on Midgard or to return you to Asgard. We'll be sleeping, but there will be room beside our dreams for yours. And when I wake, I shall look for you, my son."

Thor's great hand was firm and warm as he made his wordless farewell. Lee followed him, with words that were thick and choked, yet still faintly mocking. "So long, son. In a thousand years, I'll come down and look up Leif Svenson in the history books and read about you. You'll be there."

Leif shook his head. "Look up Leif Odinsson, Lee," he corrected, and saw Odin smile approvingly.

The others moved back to where Sudri was standing. Leif looked over Asgard again, savoring all that was good about it for one more time, and hoping to catch a glimpse of Loki or perhaps another. Then he vaulted into the saddle. Hoof-Tosser rose, and they were breasting the swirls and patterns of Bifrost.

It was easier this time, without metal on him, and there was even time for snatches of thought. He'd have to send the chest back after the apples were gone. The Aesir would need it for the next crop. And he should have brought a heavy skin mantle to protect him against the cold of Earth. But it was too late for that now. Hoof-Tosser was moving forward at a steady rolling gait, and Bifrost was only a thin mist. Then that cleared. The horse gave a sudden swoop, and went down for a gentle landing, while bright sunlight poured over them. They were back on Earth.

Leif slid from the saddle slowly, staring at his farm in surprise. It had been mid-February when he last looked through the mirror, but now it seemed more like late April. The snow was gone, and the air was warm with spring. They had landed in a small clearing in the woods not far from his house, and the trees were leafed out. Some were even blooming.

Time had made another sudden forward leap here. Or more probably, Asgard's time had slowed somehow under the stress of Ragnarok. He could never hope to understand all the complex cross-effects of the dimensional separations, though there must be a logic to them somewhere. Anyhow, Fimbulwinter was long past, and the Earth was already recovering.

Hoof-Tosser nickered again and touched his arm with a soft muzzle. Leif rubbed it, smiling faintly. "Go on, back to Asgard, Hoof-Tosser. This is no world for flying horses as long as men go on building anti-aircraft guns. Sometime I'll summon you down again, and we'll take a ride at night over safe territory. Okay?

The horse blew its breath sharply through its nostrils, shook its head, arched its neck, and was suddenly lifting and vanishing in a rainbow of color. Leif turned up the trail, coming out on fallow land. He stopped and smelled the dirt, rubbing it out over the palm of his hand. It should have been plowed and planted, though it was still a trifle too damp. And the dead wood back there should be pruned away. There'd be work enough for him, and he needed it.

"Hi, Leif!"

He looked up to see Faulkner working on a tractor. There was no real cordiality in the man's voice, but the acceptance seemed natural enough. "Heard you'd be back. I've got the accounts all ready for you to look at. How about going over them later tonight?"

"Fine," Leif told him. Then he paused. "That is, if I've still got enough in the bank to pay you. Otherwise…"

Faulkner frowned in surprise. "You mean Mr. Laufeyson didn't tell you? Well, I'll be darned. Hey, Luke!"

Loki came out of one of the smaller buildings, dressed in working clothes and smeared with tractor grease. He nodded to Leif, drawing him out of Faulkner's hearing.

"I paid him a year in advance. I figured you could use the help, and he needs enough to buy a better farm than the little place he had."

"Using what for money?"

"Money isn't hard to get when one uses the mirror to spy out things from Asgard." Loki grinned lazily, stretching himself contentedly. "And stop looking surprised at finding me here. When I saw you were going to win, I decided sleeping for a thousand years wasn't to my fancy."

They climbed the steps onto the porch, pushed through the screen door, and were in the old, familiar living room. After the great halls of Asgard, it seemed tiny and cramped. But there was a welcome odor of cooking food from the kitchen. Leif started toward it, then paused, studying Loki with a sudden stirring of doubt.

"You're not the type to settle down to farming," he accused.

"I might say the same for you, my heroic protégé," Loki said. He chuckled and picked up a paper from the table. "They're rebuilding and moving ahead here, Leif. They've even found an atomic rocket fuel! They thought Fimbuljahr was a new ice-age and were looking for a way to settle on Venus. Now they're going to explore every world in the system, and I've got money enough here to bribe passage for us. Venus, Mars, Jupiter, your moon! Do you realize it has been fifty thousand years since I explored a new world?"

The odor of food was stronger, and there was a clatter of pots and pans. Leif went through the dining room toward the kitchen. He was inside before the full shock hit him.

She turned slowly as he entered, pulling the apron up over her head. There was a hint of a smile on her mouth, but her eyes were uncertain. She took a step forward doubtfully, as if waiting for his reaction.

"Fulla! Oh, you fool!"

She was in his arms, almost crying as she pressed against him. "Fool yourself, Leif Odinsson! Did you really think I'd let you leave me when Hoof-Tosser knew the way here? I kept out a few apples, too—enough for us to have two months more together, or perhaps even three, before I change!"

Then she cried out as he unbuckled the chest and put it on the table. She tore back the cover and stared inside, incredulously. "All of them! Enough for years…for us to have sons here before I go back!"

"Better than that, Fulla!" Loki's voice drifted in from the doorway, and Leif looked up to see him standing with his arm about Gail Faulkner in familiar possession. "Come on outside, you two. I've got something worth seeing as a reunion surprise for you."

He picked up one of the apples from the chest and began munching on it carelessly, paying no heed to Fulla's gasp at the waste. He led them around the house, where a new building stood with glassed roof and sides facing the sun.

"When I learned about grafting from your books, Leif, I hadn't forgotten the long years of sleep," he said. "So I brought back a few cuttings and had an expert work on them. There are ten trees there, and all will bear Asgard fruit."

Leif looked at them, shaking his head. "They're too big for one season. And they're blooming."

"Ummm. I expected that. They're filled with the vigor of passage through Bifrost, and they're on Earth now, where plants are supposed to bloom every year. So they bloom. Long before your chest is empty, Fulla, these will be bearing in plenty."

"But…" It was coming too fast, and Leif could no longer adjust his ideas to the facts. Then another suspicion crossed his mind, and he swung toward Loki.

"Don't worry." Loki tossed the apple core onto the grass and met Leif's gaze easily. "None will go back to Asgard by my efforts. I was never fond enough of the Aesir traditions to want them imposed on this world."

He tucked Gail's arm into his own and moved back to the house, winking at Leif and leaving him alone with Fulla.

She linked her hand in his, her figure slim and golden in the sunlight as they stood looking at the little trees. She dropped down, running her fingers through the soil, watching it as it packed into a loose ball in her hands.

Leif Odinsson reached across her arm, pulling out a stalk of quack grass that was invading the plot. He grimaced. He'd be fighting that instead of giants, from now on. Giants were killable, and they stayed dead. But quack grass and weeds were enemies that never ceased and no truce was possible with them.

"We'll have to be married here, Fulla," he told her. "It wouldn't be right to have our children think we're fallen gods, just because we didn't go through the right formalities. Or are you willing to be a simple farmer's wife?"

"Oh, Leif! But Loki said you'd be going on the rockets..."

He shook his head. "Loki's got me wrong. I'm not a hero now, my dear."

But it was good to have been one, he realized. Every man should have a chance to kill a few giants, win his girl, and be a god for a while—and perhaps most men could, if they could put aside their fears long enough to try. It was comforting to have the fears behind: to need no quest for grails beyond the horizon, and not to envy those who found worlds waiting for exploration. It would be good to settle down now to a simple life where no weight of godhood rested on him.

Of course, some day when they were older and their children were grown—when the rebuilding Earth had left them behind in its forward race...

He put the thought aside and turned his mind back to Fulla. "I'm just what I said—a plain, old-fashioned dirt farmer. Do you mind?"

She showed him she didn't as they settled down onto the grass, letting the warm sun shine on them. It was good to be back, and for the moment he was content.

THE ONE-EYED MAN

A blank-faced zombie moved aside as Jimmy Bard came out of the Dictator's office, but he did not notice it; and his own gesture of stepping out of the way of the worried, patrolling adult guards was purely automatic. His tall, well-muscled body went on doing all the things long habit had taught it, while his mind churned inside him, rebelling hopelessly at the inevitable.

For a moment, the halls were free of the countless guards, and Jimmy moved suddenly to one of the walls, making quick, automatic motions with his hands. There was no visible sign of change in the surface, but he drew a deep breath and stepped forward; it was like breasting a strong current, but then he was inside and in a narrow passageway, one of the thousands of secret corridors that honeycombed the whole monstrous castle.

Here there could be no adults to remind him of what he'd considered his deficiencies, nor of the fact that those deficiencies were soon to be eliminated. The first Dictator Bard had shared the secret of the castle with none save the murdered men who built it; and death had prevented his revealing it even to his own descendants. No tapping would ever reveal that the walls were not the thick, homogenous things they seemed, for tapping would set off alarms and raise stone segments where needed, to make them as solid as they appeared. It was Jimmy's private kingdom, and one where he could be bedeviled only by his own thoughts.

But today, those were trouble enough. Morbid fascination with them drove him forward through the twisting passages until he located a section of the wall that was familiar, and he pressed his palm against it. For a second, it seemed cloudy, and then was transparent, as the energies worked on it, letting vibration through in one direction only. He did not notice the quiet sounds of those in the room beyond but riveted his eyes on the queer headpieces worn by the two girls and single boy within.

Three who had reached their twelfth birthday today and were about to become adults—or zombies! Those odd headpieces were electronic devices that held all the knowledge of a complete, all-embracing education, and they were now working silently, impressing that knowledge onto the minds of their wearers at some two hundred million impulses a second, grooving it permanently into those minds. The children who had entered with brains filled only with the things of childhood would leave with all the information they could ever need, to go out into the world as full adults, if they had withstood the shock of education. Those who failed to withstand it would still leave with the same knowledge, but the character and personality would be gone, leaving them wooden-faced, soul-less zombies.

Once Jimmy had sat in one of those chairs, filled with all the schemes and ambitions of a young rowdy about to become a man. But that time, nothing had happened! He could remember the conferences, the scientific attempts to explain his inability to absorb information from the compellor Aaron Bard had given the world, and his own tortured turmoil at finding himself something between an adult and a zombie, useless and unwanted in a world where only results counted. He had no way of knowing, then, that all the bitter years of adjusting to his fate and learning to survive in the contemptuous world were the result of a fake. It was only within the last hour that he had discovered that.

"Pure fake, carefully built up!" His Dictator father had seemed proud of that, even over the worry and desperation that had been on his face these last few days. "The other two before you who didn't take were just false leads, planted to make your case seem plausible; same with the half dozen later cases. You'd have burned—turned zombie, almost certainly. And you're a Bard, someday to dictate this country! I took the chance that if we waited until you grew older, you'd pass, and managed to use blank tapes… Now I can't wait any longer. Hell's due to pop, and I'm not ready for it, but if I can surprise them, present you as an adult… Be back here at six sharp, and I'll have everything ready for your education."

Ten years before, those words would have spelled pure heaven to him. But now the scowl deepened on his forehead as he slapped off the one-way transparency. He'd learned a lot about this world in those ten years and had seen the savage ruthlessness of the adults. He'd seen no wisdom, but only cunning and cleverness come from the Bard psychicompellors.

"Damn Aaron Bard!"

"Amen!" The soft word came sighing out of the shadows beside the boy, swinging him around with a jerk. Another, in here! Then his eyes were readjusting to the pale, bluish glow of the passages, and he made out the crouched form of an elderly man, slumped into one of the corners. That thin, weary figure with the bitter mouth and eyes could never be a castle guard, however well disguised, and Jimmy breathed easier, though the thing that might be a weapon in the hands of the other centered squarely on him.

The old man's voice trembled faintly, and there were the last dregs of bitterness in it. "Aaron Bard's damned, all right… I thought the discovery of one-way transparency was lost, though, along with controlled interpenetrability of matter-stuff around which to build a whole new science! And yet, that's the answe. For three days, I've been trying to find a trapdoor or sliding panel, boy, and all the time the trick lay in matter that could be made interpenetrable. Amusing to you?"

"No, sir." Jimmy held his voice level and quite normal. A grim ability to analyze any situation had been knocked into him during the years of his strangeness in a world that did not tolerate strangeness, and he saw that the man was close to cracking. He smiled quietly—and moved without facial warning, with the lightning reaction he had forced himself to learn, ripping the weapon out of weakened hands. His voice was still quiet. "I don't know how you know those things, nor care. The important thing is to keep you from letting others know, and…"

Sudden half-crazed laughter cut off his words. "Go back to the others and tell them? Go back and be tortured again? They'd love that. Aaron Bard's come back to tell us about some more of his nice discoveries! So sweet of you to call, my dear… I'm damned, all right, by my own reputation."

"But Aaron Bard's been dead eighty years! His corpse is preserved in a glass coffin on exhibition; I've seen it myself." And yet there was more than simple insanity here; the old man had known the two secrets which were discovered by Aaron Bard and which his son, the first Dictator, had somehow managed to find and conceal for his own ends after the inventor's death in an explosion. Those secrets had been built into the palace as part of the power of his Dictatorship, until they had been lost with his death. But the old man was speaking again, his voice weak and difficult.

"What does a mere eighty-year span mean, or a figure of wax in a public coffin? The real body they held in sterile refrigeration, filled with counter-enzymes…my own discovery, again! You know of it?"

Jimmy nodded. A Russian scientist had found safe revival of dogs possible even after fifteen minutes of death; with later development, men had been operated on in death, where it served better than anesthesia, and revived again. The only limit had been the time taken by the enzymes of the body to begin dissolving the tissues; and with the discovery by Aaron Bard of a counteracting agent, there had ceased to be any theoretical limit to safe revival. Dying soldiers in winter had injected ampules of it and been revived days or weeks later, where the cold had preserved them.

He said, "But—eighty years!"

"Why not—when my ideas were still needed, when my last experiment dealt with simple atomic power, rather than the huge, cumbersome U-235 method? Think what it would mean to an army! My son did—he was very clever at thinking of such things. Eighty years, until they could perfect their tissue regrowing methods and dare to revive my body." He laughed again, an almost noiseless wracking of his exhausted shoulders, and there was the hint of delirious raving in his voice now, though the words were still rational.

"I was so pathetically grateful and proud when they revived me. I was always gratefully proud of my achievements, you know, and what they could do for humanity. But the time had been too long—my brain only seemed normal. It had deteriorated, and I couldn't remember all I should; when I tried too hard, there were strange nightmare periods of half insanity. And their psychological torture to rip the secret from me didn't help. Two months of that, boy! They told me my name was almost like a god's in this world, and then they stopped at nothing to get what they wanted from that god! And at last I must have gone mad for a time; I don't remember, but somehow I must have escaped—I think I remember something about an air shaft. And then I was here, lost in the maze, unable to get out. But I couldn't be here, could I, if the only entrance was through interpenetrable stone panels that I couldn't remember how to energize?"

"Easy, sir." Jimmy slipped an arm under the trembling body of Aaron Bard and lifted him gently. "You could, all right. There's one out of order, in constant interpenetrable condition in an old air shaft. That's how I first found all this, years ago... There's some soup I can heat in my rooms, and you won't have to go back to them."

He might as well do one decent and human thing, while his mind was still his own, untouched by the damnable education machine. And seeing this bitter, suffering old man, he could no longer hate Aaron Bard for inventing it. The man had possessed a mind of inconceivable scope and had brought forth inventions in all fields as a cat brings forth kittens, but their misuse was no fault of his.

And suddenly it occurred to him that here in his arms was the reason for the desperation his father felt. They couldn't know of the interpenetrable panel, and the search that had undoubtedly been made and failed could have only one answer to them; he must have received outside help from some of the parties constantly plotting treason. With the threat of simple atomic power in such hands, no wonder his Dictator father was pulling all his last desperate tricks to maintain the order of things! Jimmy shook his head; it seemed that everything connected with Aaron Bard led to the position he was in and the inevitable education he must face. For a brief moment he hesitated, swayed by purely personal desires; then his hand moved out to the panel, and he was walking through into his own room, the aged figure still in his arms.

Later, when the old scientist had satisfied some of the needs of his body and was sitting on the bed, smoking, his eyes wandered slowly over the rows of books on the shelves about the room, and his eyebrows lifted slightly. "*The Age of Reason*, even! The first books I've seen in this world, Jimmy!"

"Nobody reads much, anymore, so they don't miss them at the old library. People prefer 'vision for amusement and the compellor tapes if they need additional information. I started trying to learn things from them and reading grew to be a habit."

"Um. So, you're another one-eyed man?"

"Eh?"

Bard shrugged, and the bitterness returned to his mouth. "'In the country of the blind, the one-eyed man is—killed!' Wells wrote a story about it. Where—when—I came from, men had emotional eyes to their souls, and my guess is that you've been through enough hell to develop your own. But this world is blind to such things. They don't want people to see. It's the old rule of the pack: Thou shalt conform! Jimmy, how did all this come to be?"

Jimmy frowned, trying to put it into words. The start had probably been when Aaron Bard tried his newly invented psychicompellor on his son. The boy had liked that way of learning, and stolen other experimental tapes, building with his cold, calculating little brain toward the future already. Unerringly, he'd turned to the army, apparently sensing the coming war, and making the most of it when it came. Fifteen years of exhausting, technological warfare had let him introduce the educator to furnish the technical men needed and had seen him bring forth stolen secret of his father after stolen secret, once the accidental death of Bard had left him alone in possession of Bard's files. With the war's end, the old education system was gone, and boys of twelve were serving as technicians at home until they could be replaced for active duty when old enough.

Those same boys, grown to men and desiring the same things he did, had made possible his move from General to President, and finally to Dictator. He'd even adopted the psychicompellor as his heraldic device. And the ever-increasing demands of technology made going back to old methods impossible and assured him a constant supply of young "realists." Bard interrupted. "Why? It would have been hard—getting an education was always difficult and becoming worse, which is why I tried to make the compellor—but it would have been worth it when they saw where it led. After all, without such help I managed to find a few things—even if they turned out to be Frankenstein monsters!"

"But you depended on some odd linkage of simple facts for results, and most men can't; they need a multitude of facts. And even then, we still follow you by rote in some things!"

"Too easy knowledge. They aren't using it—when they get facts, they don't have the habits of hard thinking needed to utilize them. I noticed the meager developments of new fields... But when they began making these—uh—zombies..."

Jimmy punched a button and nodded toward the creature that entered in answer. It began quietly clearing the room, removing the evidence of Bard's meal, while the scientist studied it. "There's one. He knows as much as any adult, but he has no soul, no emotions, you might say. Tell him to do something, and he will—but he won't even eat without orders."

"Permanent mechanical hypnosis," Bard muttered, and there was hell in his eyes. Then his mouth hardened, while the eyes grew even grimmer. "I never foresaw that, but—you're wrong, and it makes it even worse! You—uh—4719, answer my questions. Do you have emotions such as hatred, fear, or a sense of despair?"

Jimmy started to shake his head, but the zombie answered dully before him. "Yes, master, all those!"

"But you can't connect them with your actions—is that right? You're two people, one in hell and unable to reach the other?"

The affirmative answer was in the same dull tone again, and the zombie turned obediently and left at Bard's gesture. Jimmy wiped sudden sweat from his forehead. He'd been hoping before that he might fail the compellor education as a release, but this would be sheer, unadulterated hell! And the psychologists must know this, even though they never mentioned it.

"And ten percent of us are zombies! But only a very few at first, until the need for ever more knowledge made the shock of education greater. By then—the world had accepted such things; and some considered them a most useful by-product, since they made the best possible workers." His own voice grew more bitter as he forced it on with the history lesson, trying to forget the new and unwelcome knowledge.

Bard's son had built the monstrous castle with its secret means for spying and had fled into the passages with his private papers to die when his son wrested control from him. It was those moldy papers that had shown Jimmy the secret of escape when he'd stumbled into the labyrinth first. After that, the passage of Dictatorship from father to son had been peaceful enough and taken for granted. On the whole, there had been little of the deliberate cruelty of the ancient Nazi regime, and the dictatorial powers, while great, were not absolute. The people were used to it—after all, they were products of the compellor, and a ruthless people, best suited by dictatorial government.

Always the compellor! Jimmy hesitated for a moment, and then plunged into the tale of his own troubles. "So I'm to be made into a beast, whether I like it or not," he finished. "Oh, I could turn you in and save myself. If I were an adult, I would! That's why I hate it, even though I might like it then. It wouldn't be me—it'd be just another adult, carrying my name, doing all the things I've learned to hate. I can save myself from becoming one of them—by becoming one!"

"*Requiescat in pace*! Rest the dead in peace. If you wake them, they may learn they've made a ghastly mess of the world and may even find themselves ruining the only person in all the world whom they like!" Aaron Bard shook his head, wrinkles of concentration cutting over the lines of pain. "The weapon you took from me isn't exactly harmless. Sometime, during my temporary insanity, I must have remembered the old secret, since I made it then, and it's atom-powered. Maybe, without a dictator—"

"No! He's weak, but he's no worse than the others; I couldn't let you kill my father!"

"No, I suppose you couldn't; anyhow, killing people isn't usually much of a solution. Jimmy, are you sure there's any danger of your being made like the others?"

"I've seen the results!"

"But have you? The children are given no education or discipline until they're twelve, and then suddenly filled with knowledge, for which they haven't been prepared, even if preadolescents can be prepared for all that—which I don't believe. Even in my day, in spite of some discipline and training, twelve-year-old boys were little hoodlums, choosing to group together into gangs; wild, savage barbarians, filled with only their own egotism; pack-hunting animals, not yet civilized. Not cruel, exactly, but thoughtless, ruthless as we've seen this world is. Maybe with the sudden new flood of knowledge for which they never worked, they make good technicians; but that spurious, forced adulthood might very well discourage any real maturity; when the whole world considers them automatic adults, what incentive have they to mature?"

Jimmy thought back over his early childhood, before the education fizzle, and it was true that he and the other boys had been the egocentric little animals Bard described; there had been no thought of anything beyond their immediate whims and wants, and no one to tell them that the jungle rule for survival of the fittest should be tempered with decency and consideration for others. But the books had taught him that there had been problem children and boy-gangs before the compellor—and they had mostly outgrown it. Here, after education, they never changed; and while the pressure of society now resisted any attempt on their part to change, that wasn't the explanation needed; other ages had developed stupid standards, but there had always been those who refused them before.

"Do you believe that, sir?"

The old man shrugged slightly. "I don't know. I can't be sure. Maybe I'm only trying to justify myself. Maybe the educator does do something to the mind, carefully as I designed it to carry no personal feelings to the subject. And while I've seen some of the people, I haven't seen enough of the private life to judge; you can't judge, because you never knew normal people… When I invented it, I had serious doubts about it, for that matter. They still use it as I designed it—exactly?"

"Except for the size of the tapes."

"Then there's a wave form that will cancel out the subject's sensitivity, blanket the impulse, if broadcast within a few miles. If I could remember it—if I had an electronics laboratory where I could try it—maybe your fake immunity to education could be made real."

Relief washed over the younger man, sending him to his feet and to the panel. "There is a laboratory. The first Dictator had everything installed for an emergency, deep underground in the passages. I don't know how well stocked it is, but I've been there."

He saw purpose and determination come into the tired face, and Aaron Bard was beside him as the panel became passable. Jimmy turned through a side way that led near the Senatorial section of the castle. On impulse he turned aside and motioned the other forward. "If you want an idea of our private life, take a look at our Senators and judge for yourself."

The wall became transparent to light and sound in one direction, and they were looking out into one of the cloakrooms of the Senate Hall. One of the middle-aged men was telling a small audience of some personal triumph of his: "Their first kid—burned—just a damned zombie! I told her when she turned me down for that pimple-faced goon that I'd fix her and I did. I spent five weeks taking the kid around on the sly, winning his confidence. Just before education, I slipped him the dope in candy! You know what it does when they're full of that and the educator starts in."

Another grinned. "Better go easy telling about it; some of us might decide to turn you in for breaking the laws you helped write against using the stuff that way."

"Hell, you can't prove it. I'm not dumb enough to give you birds anything you could pin on me. Just to prove I'm the smartest man in this bunch, I'll let you in on something. I've been doing a little thinking on the Dictator's son…"

"Drop it, Pete, cold! I was with a bunch that hired some fellows to kill the monkey a couple years ago—and you can't prove that, either! We had keys to his door and everything; but he's still around, and the thugs never came back. I don't know what makes, but no other attempt has worked. The Dictator's got some tricks up his sleeve, there."

Jimmy shut the panel off and grinned. "I don't sleep anywhere near doors, and there's a section of the floor that can be made interpenetrable, with a ninety-foot shaft under it. That's why I wangled that particular suite out of my father."

"These are the Senators?" Bard asked.

"Some of the best ones." Jimmy went on, turning on a panel now and again, and Bard frowned more strongly after each new one. Some were plotting treason, others merely talking. Once something like sympathy for the zombies was expressed, but not too strongly. Jimmy started to shut the last panel off when a new voice started.

"Blane's weakling son is dead. Puny little yap couldn't take the climate and working with all the zombies in the mines; committed suicide this morning."

"His old man couldn't save him from that, eh? Good. Put it into the papers, will you? I want to be sure the Dictator's monkey gets full details. They were thick for a while, you know."

Jimmy's lips twisted as he cut off suddenly. "The only partly human person I ever knew—the one who taught me to read. He was a sickly boy, but his father managed to save him from euthanasia, somehow. Probably he went around with me for physical protection, since the others wouldn't let him alone. Then they shipped him to some mines down in South America, to handle zombie labor."

"Euthanasia? Nice word for killing off the weak. Biologically, perhaps such times as these may serve a useful purpose, but I'd rather have the physically weak around than those who treat them that way. Jimmy, I think if my trick doesn't work and the educator does things to you it shouldn't, I'll kill you before I kill myself!"

Jimmy nodded tightly. Bard wasn't the killing type, but he hoped he'd do it, if such a thing occurred. Now he hurried, wasting no more time in convincing the other of the necessity to prevent such a change in him. He located the place he wanted and stepped in, pressed a switch on the floor, and set the lift to dropping smoothly downward.

"Power is stolen, but cleverly, and no one has suspected. There are auxiliary fuel-batteries, too. The laboratory power will be the same. And here we are."

He pointed to the room, filled with a maze of equipment of all kinds, neatly in order, but covered with dust and dirt from long disuse. Aaron Bard looked at it slowly, with a wry grin.

"Familiar, Jimmy. My son apparently copied it from my old laboratory, where he used to fiddle around sometimes, adapting my stuff to military use. With a little decency, he'd have been a good scientist; he was clever enough."

Jimmy watched, some measure of hope coming to him, as the old man began working. He cleared the tables of dust with casual flicks of a cloth and began, his hands now steady. Wires, small tubes, coils, and various other electronic equipment came from the little boxes and drawers, though some required careful search. Then his fingers began the job of assembling and soldering them into a plastic case about the size of a muskmelon, filled almost solidly as he went along.

"That boy who taught you how to read—was he educated at the age of twelve?"

"Of course—it's compulsory. Everyone has to be. Or—" Jimmy frowned, trying to remember more clearly; but he could only recall vague hints and phrases from bits of conversation among Blane's enemies. "There was something about falsified records during the euthanasia judgment proceedings, I think, but I don't know what records. Does it matter?"

Bard shrugged, scribbling bits of diagrams on a scrap of dirty paper before picking up the soldering iron again. "I wish I knew… Umm? In that fifteen-year war, when they first began intensive use of the compellor, they must have tried it on all types and ages. Did any scientist check on variations due to such factors? No, they wouldn't! No wonder they don't develop new fields. How about a book of memoirs by some soldier who deals with personalities?"

"Maybe, but I don't know. The diary of the first Dictator might, if it could be read, but when I tried after finding it, I only got hints of words here and there. It's in some horrible code—narrow strips of short, irregularly spaced letter groups, pasted in. I can't even figure what kind of a code it is, and there's no key."

"Key's in the library, Jimmy, if you'll look up Brak-O-Type-machine shorthand. He considered ordinary typing inefficient; one time when I thoroughly agreed with him. Damn!" Bard sucked on the thumb where a drop of solder had fallen and stared down at the tight-packed parts. He picked up a tiny electrolytic condenser, studied the apparatus, and put it down again doubtfully. Then he sat motionlessly, gazing down into the half-finished object.

The work, which had progressed rapidly at first, was now beginning to go more slowly, with long pauses while the older man thought. And the pauses lengthened. Jimmy slipped out and up the lift again, to walk rapidly down a corridor that would lead him to the rear of one of the restaurants of the castle. The rats had been blamed for a great deal at that place, and they were in for more blame as Jimmy slid his hands back into the corridors with coffee and food in them.

Bard gulped the coffee gratefully as he looked up to see the younger man holding out the food, but he only sampled that. His hands were less sure again. "Jimmy, I don't know—I can't think. I get so far, and everything seems clear; then—*pfft*! It's the same as when I first tried to remember the secret of atomic power; there are worn places in my mind-eroded by eighty years of death. And when I try to force my thoughts across them, they stagger and reel."

"Grandfather Bard, you've got to finish it! It's almost five, and I have to report back at six!"

Bard rubbed his wrinkled forehead with one hand, clenching and opening the other. For a time, then, he continued to work busily, but there were long quiet intervals. "It's all here, except this one little section. If I could put that in right, it'd work—but if I make a mistake, it'll probably blow out, unless it does nothing." Jimmy stared at his watch. "Try it."

"You solder it; my hands won't work anymore." Bard slipped off the stool, directing the boy's hands carefully. "If I could be sure of making it by going insane, as I did the atom-gun, I'd even force my mind through those nightmares again. But I might decide to do almost anything else, instead... No, that's the antenna—one end remains free."

The hands of the watch stood at ten minutes of six as the last connection was made and Bard plugged it into the socket near the floor. Then the tubes were warming up. There was no blowout, at least; the tubes continued to glow, and a tiny indicator showed radiation of some form coming from the antenna. Jimmy grinned, relief stronger in him, but the older man shook his head doubtfully as they went back to the lift again.

"I don't know whether it's working right, son. I put that last together by mental rule of thumb, and you shouldn't work that way in delicate electronic devices, where even two wires accidentally running beside each other can ruin things! But at least we can pray. And as a last resort—well, I still have the atom-pistol."

"Use it, if you need to! I'll take you to the back wall of my father's inner office, and you can stay there watching while I go around the long way. And use it quickly, because I'll know you're there!"

It took him three tries to find a hallway that was empty of the guards and slip out, but he was only seconds late as his father opened the door and let him in; the usual secretaries and guards were gone, and only the chief psychologist stood there, his small stock of equipment set up. But the Dictator hesitated.

"Jimmy, I want you to know I have to do this, even though I don't know whether you have any better chance of passing it now than when you were a kid—that's just my private hunch, and the psychologist here thinks I'm wrong. But—well, something I was counting on is probably stolen by conspiracy, and there's a helluva war brewing in Eurasia against us, which we're not ready for; the oligarchs have something secret that they figure will win. It's all on a private tape I'll give you. I don't know how much help you'll be, but seeing you suddenly normal will back up the bluff I'm planning, at least. We Bards have a historic destiny to maintain, and I'm counting on you to do your part. You must pass!"

Jimmy only half heard it. He was staring at the headpiece, looking something like a late-style woman's hat with wires leading to a little box on the table, and varicolored spools of special tape. For a second, as it clamped down over his face, he winced, but then stood it in stiff silence. In the back of his mind, something tried to make itself noticed—but as he groped for it, only a vague, uneasy feeling remained. Words and something about the psychologist's face...

He heard the snap of the switch, and then his mind seemed to freeze, though sounds and sights still registered. But he knew that the device in the room so far below had failed! The pressure on his brain was too familiar by description; the Bard psychicompellor was functioning. For a second, before full impact, he tried to tear it off, but something else seemed to control his mind, and he sat rigidly, breathing hard, but unable to stop it. His thoughts died down, became torpid, while the machine went on driving its two hundred million impulses into his brain every second, doing things that science still could not understand, but could use.

He watched stolidly as the spools were finished, one by one, until his father produced one from a safe and watched it used, then smashed it. The psychologist bent, picked up one last one, and attached it... The face of the man was familiar... "Like to have the brat in front of a burner like those we use in zombieing criminals..."

Then something in his head seemed to slither, like feet slipping on ice. Numbed and dull of mind, he still gripped at himself, and his formerly motionless hands were clenching at the arms of the chair. Something gnawing inside, a queer distortion, that... Was this what a zombie felt, while its mind failed under education?

The psychologist bent then, removing the headset. "Get up, James Bard!" But as Jim still sat, surprise came over his face, masked instantly by a look of delighted relief. "So you're no zombie?"

Jim arose then, rubbing his hands across his aching forehead, and managed to smile. "No," he said quietly. "No, I'm all right. *I'm perfectly all right!* Perfectly."

"Praise be, Jimmy." The Dictator relaxed slowly into his chair. "And now you know... What's the matter?"

Jim couldn't tell him of the assurance necessary to keep Aaron Bard from firing, but he held his face into a pleasant smile in spite of the pain in his head as he turned to face his father. He knew now—everything. Quietly, unobtrusively, all the things he hadn't known before were there, waiting for his mind to use, along with all the things he had seen and all the conversations he had spied upon in secret.

He had knowledge—and a mind trained to make the most of it. The habits of thinking he had forced upon himself were already busy with the new information; even the savage, throbbing pain couldn't stop that. Now he passed his hand across his head deliberately and nodded to the outer office. "My head's killing me, Father. Can't I use the couch out there?"

"For a few minutes, I guess. Doctor, can't you give the boy something?"

"Maybe. I'm not a medical doctor, but I can fix the pain, I think." The psychologist was abstract, but he turned out. The Dictator came last, and they were out of the little room, into the larger one where no passages pierced the walls, and no shot could reach him.

The smile whipped from the boy's face then, and one of his hands snapped out, lifting a small flame gun from his father's hip with almost invisible speed. It came up before the psychologist could register the emotions that might not yet have begun, and the flame washed out, blackening clothes and flesh and leaving only a limp, charred body on the floor.

Jim kicked it aside. "Treason. He had a nice little tape in there, made out by two people of totally opposite views, in spite of the law against it. Supposed to burn me into a zombie. It would have, except that I'd already studied both sides pretty well, and it raised Ned for a while, even then. Here's your gun, Father."

"Keep it!" The first real emotion Jim had ever seen on his father's face was there now, and it was fierce pride. "I never saw such beautiful gun work, boy! Or such a smooth job of handling a snake! Thanks be, you aren't soft and weak, as I thought. No more emotional nonsense, eh?"

"No more. I'm cured. And at the meeting of the Senators you've called, maybe we'll have a surprise for them. You go on down, and I'll catch up as soon as I can get some amidopyrene for this headache. Somehow, I'll think of something to stop the impeachment they're planning."

"Impeachment! That bad? But how—why didn't you—"

"I did try to tell you, years ago. But though I knew every little treason plot they were cooking then, you were too busy to listen to a nonadult, and I didn't try again. Now, though, it'll be useful. See you outside assembly, unless I'm late."

He grinned mirthlessly as his father went down the hall and away from him. The look of pride in his too-heavy face wouldn't have stayed there if he'd known just how deep in treason some of the fine Senator friends were. It would take a dozen miracles to pull them through. Jim found the panel he wanted, looked to be sure of privacy, and slipped through, tracing quickly down the corridor.

But Aaron Bard wasn't to be found. For a second, he debated more searching, but gave it up; there was no time, and he could locate the old man later. It wasn't important that he be found at the moment. Jim shrugged and slipped into one of the passages that would serve as a shortcut to the great assembly room. The headache was already disappearing, and he had no time to bother with it.

They were already beginning session when he arrived, even so, and he slipped quietly through the Dictator's private entrance, making his way unnoticed to the huge desk, behind a jade screen that would hide him from the Senators and yet permit him to watch. He had seen other sessions before, but they had been noisy, bickering affairs, with the rival groups squabbling and shouting names. Today there was none of that. They were going through the motions, quite plainly stalling for time, and without interest in the routine. This meeting was a concerted conspiracy to depose the Dictator, though only the few leaders of the groups knew that Eurasian bribery and treason were the real reasons behind it.

It had been in the making for years, while those leaders carefully built up the ever-present little hatreds and discontents. Jim's status had been used to discredit his father, though the man's own weaknesses had been more popular in distorted versions. As Jim looked, he saw that the twelve cunning men lured to treason by promises of being made American Oligarchs, though supposedly heading rival groups, were all still absent; that explained the stalling. Something was astir, and Jim had a hunch that the psychologist's corpse would have been of no little interest to them. The two honest group leaders were in session, grim and quiet; then, as he looked, the twelve came in, one by one, from different entrances. Their faces showed no great sense of defeat.

Naturally. The Dictator had no chance; he had tried to rule by dividing the now-united groups and by family prestige and had kept afloat so long as they were not ready to strike; the methods would not stand any strain, much less this attack. He had already muffed one attack opportunity while the leaders were out. A strong man would have cut through the stalling and taken the initiative; a clever orator, schooled in the dramatics and emotions of a Webster or a Borah might even have controlled them. But the Dictator was weak, and the compellor did not produce great oratory; that was incompatible with such emotional immaturity.

But the Dictator had finally been permitted to speak, now. He should have begun with the shock of Jim's adulthood to snap them out of their routine thoughts, built up the revival of Aaron Bard and his old atomic power work, to make them wonder, and then swept his accusations over them in short, hard blows. Instead, he was tracing the old accomplishments of the Bard Family, stock, familiar phrases with no meaning left in them.

Jim sat quietly; it was best that his father should learn his own weakness, here and now. He peered down to watch the leading traitor, and the expression on the man's face snapped his head around, even as his father saw the same thing and stopped talking.

An arm projected from the left wall, waving a dirty scrap of paper at them, and Jim recognized the sheet Bard had used for his diagrams. Now the arm suddenly withdrew, to be replaced by the grinning head of Aaron Bard—but not the face Jim had seen; this one contained sheer lunacy, the teeth bared, the eyes protruding, and the muscles of the neck bunched in mad tension! As Jim watched, the old man emerged fully into the room and began stalking steadily down the aisles toward the Dictator's desk, the atom-gun in one hand centered squarely on Jim's father.

He had full attention, and no one moved to touch him as his feet marched steadily forward, while the scrap of paper in his hand waved and fluttered. Now his voice chopped out words and seemed to hurl them outward with physical force. "Treason! Barbarism! Heathen idolatry!"

For a second, Jim took his eyes from Bard to study his father, then to spring from the chair in a frantic leap as he saw the Dictator's nerve crack and his finger slip onto one of the secret tiny buttons on the desk. But the concealed weapon acted too quickly, though there was no visible blast from it. Aaron Bard uttered a single strangled sound and crumpled to the floor!

"Get back!" Jim wasted no gentleness on his father as he twisted around the desk to present the crowding Senators with the shock of his presence at assembly on top of their other surprise. He had to dominate now, while there was a power hiatus. He bent for a quick look. "Coagulator! Who carries an illegal coagulator here? Some one of you, because this man is paralyzed by one."

Mysteriously, a doctor appeared and nodded after a brief examination. "Coagulator, all right. His nerves are cooked from chest down, and it's spreading. Death certain in an hour or so."

"Will he regain consciousness?"

"Hard to say. Nothing I can do, but I'll try, if someone will move him to the rest room."

Jim nodded and stooped to pick up the scrawled bit of paper and the atom-gun. He had been waiting for a chance, and now fate had given it to him. The words he must say were already planned, brief and simple to produce the impact he must achieve, while the assembly was still disorganized and uncertain; if oratory could win them, now was the time for it. With a carefully stern and accusing face, he mounted the platform behind the desk. His father started to speak, then stopped in shock as Jim took the gavel, rapped for order, and began, pacing with words in a slow rhythm while measuring the intensity for his voice by the faces before him.

"Gentlemen, eighty years ago, Aaron Bard died on the eve of a great war, trying to perfect a simple atomic release that would have shortened that war immeasurably. Tomorrow you will read in your newspapers how that man's own genius preserved his body and enabled us to revive him on this, the eve of an even grimmer war.

"Now, a few moments ago, that same man gave his life again in the service of this country, killed by the illegal coagulator of some cowardly traitor. But he did not die in vain, or before he could leave us safely to find his well-earned rest. He has left his mark on many of us; on me, by giving me the adulthood that all our scientists could not; on some of you, in this piece of paper, he has left a grimmer mark...

"You saw him emerge from a solid wall, and it was no illusion, however much he chose to dramatize his entrance; the genius that was his enabled him to discover a means to search out your treason and your conspiracy in your most secret places. You heard his cry of treason! And one among you tried to silence that cry, forgetting that written notes cannot be silenced with a coagulator.

"Nor can you silence his last and greatest discovery, here in this weapon you saw him carry—portable atomic power...

"Now there will be no war; no power would commit such suicide against a nation whose men shall be equipped as ours shall be. You may be sure that the traitors among you will find no reward for their treason, now. But from them, we shall have gained. We shall know the folly of our petty, foreign-inspired hatreds. We shall know the need of cleansing ourselves of the taint of such men's leadership. We shall cease trying to weaken our government and shall unite to forge new bonds of strength, instead.

"And because of that unintended good they have done us, we shall be merciful! Those who leave our shores before the stroke of midnight shall be permitted to escape; those who prefer to choose their own death by their own hands shall not be denied that right. And for the others, we shall demand and receive the fullest measure of justice!

"In that, gentlemen, I think we can all agree."

He paused then for a brief moment, seeming to study the paper in his hand, and when he resumed, his voice was the brusque one of a man performing a distasteful task. "Twelve men—men who dealt directly with our enemies. I shall read them in the order of their importance: First, Robert Sweinend! Two days ago, at three o'clock in his secretary's office, he met a self-termed businessman named Yamamoto Tung, though he calls himself—"

Jim went on, methodically reciting the course of the meeting, tensing inside as the seconds stretched on; much more and they would know it couldn't all come from one small sheet of paper!

But Sweinend's hand moved then, and Jim's seemed to blur over the desktop. Where the Senator had been, a shaft of fire—atomic fire—seemed to hang for a second before fading into nothing. Jim put the gun back gently and watched eleven men get up from their seats and dart hastily away through the exits. Beside him, his father's face now shone with great relief and greater pride, mixed with unbelieving wonder as he stood up awkwardly to take the place the boy was relinquishing. The job had been done, and Jim had the right to follow his own inclinations.

Surprisingly to him, the still figure on the couch, was both conscious and sane, as the boy shut the door of the little room, leaving the doctor outside. Aaron Bard could not move his body, but his lips smiled. "Hello, Jimmy. That was the prettiest bundle of lies I've heard in a lot more than eighty years! I'm changing my saying; from now on, the one-eyed man is king—so long as he taps the ground with a cane!"

Jimmy nodded soberly, though most of the strain of the last hour was suddenly gone, torn away by the warm understanding of the older man and relief at not having to convince him that he was still normal, in spite of his actions since education. "You were right about the compellor; it can't change character. But I thought...after I shot the psychiatrist... How did you know?"

"I had at least twenty minutes in which to slip back and examine my son's diary, before your education would be complete." His smile deepened, as he sucked in on the cigarette that Jimmy held to his lips, and he let the smoke eddy out gently. "It took perhaps ten minutes to learn what I wanted to know. During the war, his notes are one long paean of triumph over the results on the preadolescents, dissatisfaction at those who were educated past twenty! And he knew the reason, as well as he always knew what he wanted to. Too much information on a young mind mires it down by sheer weight on untrained thoughts, even though it gives a false self-confidence. But the mature man, with his trained mind, can never be bowed down by mere information; he can use it... No, let me go on. Vindication of my compellor doesn't matter; but this is going to be your responsibility, Jimmy, and the doctor told me I'm short of time. I want to be sure... In twenty years—but that doesn't matter.

"The compellor is poison to a twelve-year-old mind, and a blessing to the adult. You can't change that overnight; but you can try, and perhaps accomplish a little. Move the age up, but carefully. By rights I should repair the damage I helped cause, but I'll have to leave it to you. Be ruthless, as you were now—more ruthless than any of them. A man who fights for right and principle should be. Tap the ground with your cane! And sometimes, when none of the blind are around, you can look up and still see the stars! Now—"

"Grandfather Bard—you never were insane in there!"

The old man smiled again. "Naturally. I couldn't look on and see the only one of my offspring that amounted to anything needing help without doing something, could I? I threw in everything I could, knowing you'd make something out of it. You did. And I'm not sorry, even though I wasn't exactly expecting—this... How long after my heart begins missing?"

"A minute or two!" Aaron Bard obviously wanted no sympathy, and the boy sensed it and held back the words, hard though he found it now. Emotions were better expressed by their hands locked together than by words.

"Good. It's a clean, painless death, and I'm grateful for it. But no more revivals! Cremate me, Jimmy, and put up a simple marker—no name, just A One-Eyed Man!"

"*Requiescat in Pace*—A One-Eyed Man! I promise!" The old head nodded faintly and relaxed, the smile still lingering. Jimmy swallowed a lump in his throat and stood up slowly with bowed head, while a tumult of sound came in from the great assembly hall. His father was finally abdicating, and they were naming him Dictator, of course. But he still stood there, motionless.

"Two such stones," he muttered finally. "And maybe someday I'll deserve the other."

www.ingramcontent.com/pod-product-compliance
Lightning Source LLC
Chambersburg PA
CBHW020145180626
46810CB00004B/1736